TALES FROM THE ORICERAN UNIVERSE

TALES FROM THE ORICERAN UNIVERSE

UNIVERSE

FANS WRITE FOR THE FANS: VOLUME 2

MICHAEL ANDERLE   TRACEY BYRNES   LISA FRETT
CHARLES TILLMAN   DOMINIC NOVIELLI
LOGAN CAIRD   T.L. GRYFEN

DISRUPTIVE IMAGINATION

LMBPN Publishing
PMB 196, 2540 South Maryland Pkwy
Las Vegas, NV 89109

First US edition, April 2019

ISBN: 978-1-64202-194-3

TALES FROM THE ORICERAN UNIVERSE

Thank you to the following JIT Readers

Mary Morris
Peter Manis
Misty Roa

If we missed anyone, please let us know!

Skyhunter Editing Team

INTRODUCTION

WRITTEN BY MARTHA CARR

In the Oriceran Universe, fans are more like friends, until some of them even become Authors. Over the past year and a half, (yes, that's all it's been), the Universe has grown to over 125 books with some great characters like Leira and YTT, and Brownstone and Shay, or Alison and Raine.

The entire universe started with one idea about gates opening gradually to let magic back into our world and a thought about what that might look like. That was all Anderle. It grew into a collaboration of Leira and Correk and that troll and quickly spread across not just one map, but two (Oriceran and the United States) with stories for readers who like fantasy, or a lot more action, even a little romance.

Today, Michael Anderle and I would like to introduce you to a new set of stories from fans just like you who have fallen in love with this world of magic and trolls and adventure.

Without further ado, because I know you want to get to reading, here is the second anthology of Fans Write for Fans. Get that Coke and Cheetos ready and settle in for a while... You have a great day of reading ahead of you.

Still more adventures to follow.

CAST IN STONE

BY TRACEY BYRNES

Lethal dark magic. A desperate gamble for survival. Decades of being trapped in a stone statue, unable to communicate... Until one emotionally-charged moment turns life on its head.

The stakes are once again life or death as an old enemy seeks to eradicate all opposition. Will light magic become the key to freedom? Or will "cast in stone" be a final fate?

DEDICATION

For everyone who's encouraged me to set the magic free, then keep following wherever it leads. You rock.

CHAPTER ONE

"It's hard *being a rock; they have such a strange sense of time—and priorities."* This was a line from a Mercedes Lackey book I'd read decades ago that stuck with me. It was both ironic and apt, considering my decades-long predicament of being trapped in a statue. A fifteen-foot-tall, lichen-spotted granite chimera located deep within a hedge-maze, to be precise.

I wasn't a chimera—or I wasn't originally, at least—but I'd spent more years than I cared to think about trapped in my current surroundings. I honestly wasn't sure I'd remember how to be human after so long but often entertained myself thinking about it. It helped me stay sane.

My musings were interrupted by faint vibrations caused by bare feet walking on the manicured grass nearby. It took me years to figure out that I could feel things through my stony aspect and even longer to gain an extremely limited measure of sight and hearing. As hard as it was to think like a stone, it was even more difficult to adapt spells so I could cast them without using physical gestures.

The vibrations grew subtly stronger as a teenage girl rounded the corner of the hedge, her walk light and fluid in spite of its quickness. Tawny, I'd heard her called, although I wasn't sure if that was a nickname due to her coloring or her real name. She was a member of House Eventide, whose hedge-maze I occupied, and a promising young witch.

I also knew, from things she'd spoken aloud while in my presence, that there were many questions about her heritage. She was a witch—already quite strong in spite of not yet being fifteen years old—but showed signs of abilities not commonly seen in her House. Her mother merely told the family—or so I gathered —to give the girl the usual training that all witches and wizards in House Eventide received.

All family members were taught both light and dark spells, ensuring a thorough magical education. Most used light magic, although a few straddled the line between light and dark. Those few were often referred to as "gray," but it wasn't a commonly accepted term. The grays were the "neutral" balance when arguments devolved into interfamily spats and feuds. The latter were short-lived, though, because House Eventide brooked no lasting dissention in its ranks. Grievances were aired and settled one way or another, ensuring that the House, as a whole, remained united and strong.

Tawny was considered neutral, although she identified as light. From what little I'd seen, her assessment was accurate. Her magic, when she'd practiced in front of—and sometimes on—me, didn't have the telltale dark taint. As a child, she'd often balked at practicing the dark spells that were part of House Eventide's collective arsenal. That changed after an *Alice In Wonderland*-type turn of events.

CHAPTER TWO

I recalled the day when she first heard my thoughts. Her look of panicked bewilderment changed to astonished wonderment as she slowly accepted that the voice in her head was real, not a figment of her imagination. I was relieved that she was young enough—she was perhaps six or seven years old at the time—to still have a child's flexible worldview. She accepted my admittedly outré story with far less difficulty than an adult would've had.

The day started like countless others. The dark chill of a late fall Virginia night slowly gave way to sunrise. Pale streaks of warmth from the first rays of light teased across my cold granite form. They grew larger and warmer as the sun continued to rise, covered me slowly, and dried the dew that blanketed my lichen-spotted form. By late morning, all but a few shadowed patches were dry.

Tawny came to the hedge-maze as she so often did, but her steps dragged, and her face was a thundercloud of angry tears mixed with rebellious despair. She'd collapsed against my base, her shoulders shaking and chest heaving as her choked sobs completely engulfed her body. My cool granite exterior was no comfort to the distraught girl, although deep within my stony prison, I wanted it to be. Subconsciously I must've tried to make it happen, although I didn't think it was possible.

Eventually, the wild storm of emotion dwindled to random, hiccupping sobs. When she'd mastered herself enough to speak, the story came tumbling out in bits and disjointed pieces. "I can't! It's dark... It hurts just to think about it... I don't want to hurt people!" Fresh sobs forced their way out. "Gramma Sophie insists I have to learn it. Mum is staying silent...*why isn't she defending me?*" The last part came out in a wail as she tried to cope with her mother's perceived betrayal.

::*Calm, little one.*:: The thought reverberated in my head, repeating itself as I tried, with every ounce of willpower I could muster, to project it to her through unyielding stone.

That's when the look on her face changed to panicked bewilderment.

She scrambled away and backed far enough to take in my entire form. "Wh-who's speaking? Am I going crazy?" She shoved a hand into her hair and pulled it as she wrapped her other arm around her middle to hug herself.

::*Calm,*:: I thought again, worked to project it, and prayed the first time hadn't been a fluke. Her eyes widened even further as she pulled her hand from her hair and wound that arm around herself as well.

"A-are y-you...the *statue?*" Her stuttering question showed she was quick to correctly put two and two together.

::*Yes.*:: I kept it simple. There was so much more to it than that, but it took everything I had to simply communicate this much. It also didn't help that my shock threatened to derail my efforts. I pressed on with the key point while I still could. ::*Learn the spell. Then you'll know how to counter it.*::

She froze. I knew by her reaction that she'd heard me. The myriad emotions that flashed across her face gave me some insight into her thoughts. Her next comment confirmed that she was spunky as well as smart.

"Great. Now I have a statue giving me advice," she muttered before continuing in conversational tones. "Let's say I learn this dark spell Gramma Sophie insists I need to know. Not that I *want* to. I don't ever want to use it. I think it'd kill me if I did. But let's say I learn it anyway. How does knowing it mean I'll know how to counter it?"

::*You'll recognize it. That means you can interrupt it or counterspell.*:: Again, I kept my thoughts as simple as possible since with each attempt to project them, my head throbbed in agony.

I watched as she worked through my answer. "Oh! I get it now." She shifted her weight and cocked her head as she looked at me—or, rather, the statue—with an oddly assessing gaze.

"It hurts you to talk to me like this, doesn't it?"

::*Yes.*:: I was stunned and wondered how she'd picked up on that.

"Here's what I'm gonna do, then. I'll go back to the house for my next set of lessons now, but I'll come back tomorrow. You rest... Wait, do statues need rest? Or do you...I don't know, exist outside all that stuff? Anyway, we can try this mind-speaking thing again when I come back. That *is* what it's called, right? No, don't answer. I'll figure it out on my own."

Her rapid flow of comments took me a few moments to process. By the time I had, she'd waved goodbye and walked out of sight. I felt the slight vibrations from her footsteps move further away, then vanish completely as she eventually reached the edge of the maze and, presumably, headed across the expanse of green lawn toward the sprawling three-story antebellum mansion in Williamsburg that House Eventide called home.

CHAPTER THREE

I'd done as Tawny recommended and rested the part of my mind that had such an unexpected workout. Statues, in general, probably don't need to rest, but human-inhabited statues are apparently a different story. While I rested, I thought through what had happened. Emotion seemed to be the trigger. There was something more to it, though... I suspected it was something about Tawny and/or her magic that played a pivotal role in my sudden ability to communicate with her. It was something I wanted to test if we were able to keep communicating.

It was late afternoon when she arrived the next day. The sun played hide-and-seek in the puffy white clouds that scudded by as a light breeze rustled the hedges. Her light footsteps drew closer and closer. Their almost-dancing rhythm bespoke the lighthearted air that accompanied her around the corner into my clearing.

She pirouetted a couple times while caroling, "Thank you!" before she settled onto the grass within sight of my carved eyes.

"I don't know if you can see me but now that I know you can communicate, it seems rude to behave as though you can't."

I chuckled silently. ::I can see...a little. I feel vibrations better.::

"Ah-ha! That's one question answered!" The look on her face was smug glee. She'd apparently been thinking and now had questions. I hoped I'd be able to answer them.

"I started learning that spell Gramma Sophie talked about. Mum told me that while she didn't like it, she was glad I'd decided to learn it. 'Knowledge is never wasted,' was the quote she used." Her lips twisted as she made a face. "It makes me feel dirty, though…like I've rolled in a sludge-filled pig sty and then coated it by swimming in an oil slick."

::Dark spells feel that way when you're a light being. Remember that you're learning it mostly to defend against it.::

"I know, I know. Still, *eww.*" She wagged her finger at me.

I chuckled at her cheeky reaction, in total agreement with her.

———

As the years passed and Tawny grew, our discussions continued and became more complex. It was still an effort for me to communicate, but we'd managed to extend the amount of time I could speak to her before the throbbing headaches that warned me I had overextended myself set in.

I'd not managed to run any kind of conclusive tests to see if my suspicions about the other catalyst for the two of us to communicate were correct, but I hadn't given up my desire to know. Unbeknownst to me at the time, Tawny was also doing research. That little tidbit came out one afternoon when she was a couple of months shy of her fifteenth birthday.

"I've looked through the House history books to see if I could figure out who you are. I mean, besides a granite chimera. Dude, why'd you choose *that* of all things? Wasn't there something else available? Because that is one messed-up creature."

Her artlessly pointed aside made me chuckle. My amusement died, and alarm raced through me as I realized that she'd ventured into dangerous territory. Did the enemy I'd fled at the time still live? If so, knowing that information would make her a target.

::Did you discover who I am?::

"No."

::Good. Don't dig further until I know if it's safe. Knowing who I am could get you killed.::

Her eyes widened. She started to speak, then closed her mouth and mimed zipping her lips shut. Moments passed. The birds chirping in the distance were the loudest sounds around us.

Then, a delicate tendril of thought reached my mind. ::Careful. You gave me a clue about who you are.::

::What?:: My stunned reaction inadvertently broadcast itself as a projected thought.

::Ha! It worked!:: Her gleeful exclamations rang through my head as she wriggled excitedly where she sat.

"I was curious, so one of the things I looked up was mind-speech. I thought, since reading the House histories is required, I might as well look for something that interested me. I found several spells for it and some recorded instances of when and why it was used. Handy stuff, although the spells have limited durations."

I was about to ask her which spells she'd found when she dropped a bombshell.

::I also found an instance where a daughter of the House gained an ability for mind-speech. She'd connected—or maybe the word was 'bonded,' the translation wasn't clear—with 'a male wizard of light persuasion who possessed unusual powers.' The entry noted that he helped defend the family when a tear leading into the World in Between opened on the northern edge of our property.::

If I weren't a statue, my jaw would've hit the ground and bounced several times. They'd recorded that? The head of family at the time—her name escaped me, but she was someone I'd once known well—had promised to keep as much detail about that incident out of their histories as possible. Then again…

::Did the histories say anything more about it?::

::Only that the person responsible for creating the tear was 'appropriately dealt with.'::

Ah. She'd kept her promise. The tear had to be mentioned, since it documented an incident that'd needed hefty magical firepower to contain and then close it, but she'd downplayed my part in it and the results of the bond as much as she could. Still, this precocious young girl had already correctly put together too many facts for my comfort.

Before I could ask any more questions, Tawny bounced to her feet. "Gramma Tatia told me about something when she learned what I was reading and suggested I try it with you. I don't know how she knew what happened, but she said it was something that 'might help in the long run.'"

::Gramma Tatia? Is that—::

Before I could say another word, Tawny somehow climbed onto my back and leaned forward, pressed her face against me, and wound her arms around my neck as far as she could reach.

::How did—::

"I climbed, boosted by a minor levitation spell. Now hush." She spoke absently, her thoughts clearly elsewhere as demonstrated by the sudden flood of warmth which enveloped my mind.

::Ah-ha! Gramma Tatia was right!:: she enthused, her thoughts clear and overlaid with all the nuances of what she was felt, thought, and—startlingly—saw. *::Now, let's see if I can teach you the same trick.::*

Wordlessly, she replayed the memory of her Gramma Tatia teaching her to connect with me in a way I hadn't thought possible, regardless of her abilities. As I studied her memory further and broke it down into the mechanics before building it back up to the cohesive whole, I realized three things. One, not many people would be able to do this. Two, Tawny was a hell of a lot more gifted than anyone realized. Three, the reason I could speak to her was that we were somehow related.

She spoke in the same moment that I came to those mind-blowing realizations. *::Try speaking with me now. Is it any easier?::*

As before, I now heard-felt-saw everything attached to the words. It was extremely disconcerting after being deprived of that type of input for so many years—something which evidently came through clearly since she giggled as I responded, *::The universe has a hell of a sense of humor.::* The thought was overlaid with myriad emotions and a whirl of almost-chaotic images as memories flew across the surface of my mind to bombard us both. I cut them off abruptly, took a deep mental breath, and focused before speaking again.

::Yes, it's much easier now. Thank you. Thank your Gramma Tatia for me as well...and ask if she'd be willing to visit me.::

Tawny started to respond, then gulped. *::Actually...you can ask her yourself.::*

My puzzlement was quickly laid to rest when a new voice spoke. "Child, what on earth are you doing astride that statue?"

"I thought it would be easier if I was in direct contact. It worked, Gramma Tatia!"

"I see. Have you tried it without being in contact?" Gramma Tatia clearly knew exactly what Tawny was talking about and guided her to take the next step in her experiment.

"No."

::Now that we've figured out how to easily communicate while touching, Tawny, let's see if we can duplicate our results without being in physical contact.:: I projected my thought to both of them since I wanted to see if both could hear me or if it was unique to Tawny and me.

Tatia's eyebrows flew upward as I spoke. "An excellent idea. Tawny, please be careful getting down!" The last was in response to the girl's vault off me and subsequent landing on the grass.

"Levitation, Gramma. I was in no danger of falling. I told you, I practice all the spells I'm taught, even when I don't like them. At least this one is fun, even though it's serious business."

I chuckled mentally. She sounded so much like me when I was her age—I had a shrewd notion her mother had much the same attitude.

"Something is amusing?" Tatia arched her eyebrow as she addressed me directly.

::*Very*.:: I addressed my next comment solely to her. ::*It seems that in some respects, the apple didn't fall very far from either of the family trees.*::

She laughed aloud and turned to her granddaughter. "Please go see Gramma Sophie. She has another spell to teach you, one which will be of benefit in the days soon to come."

Tawny began to protest but stopped as the old lady raised her hand. "I will relay whatever is spoken of here as fully as possible, but right now, your friend and I need to speak one-on-one. Go, child. I promise, what Gramma Sophie has to teach you *will* be relevant, sooner rather than later."

"Okay, I'll go. Oh, and thanks, Gramma Tatia. This was amazing!" She sent me the mental equivalent of a big hug before she turned and walked out of sight.

::*So.*::

::*It's been a long time, Tatia.*:: My thought overlapped hers as we spoke simultaneously.

::*That it has.*:: The emotional overtones that filled her comment spoke of grief, fear, anger, and weariness. ::*Much has changed, Andar, not all of it for the better.*::

I acknowledged that wordlessly.

::*Tawny is something I didn't see coming. She's strong—stronger than all of us put together, I believe, which is a truly frightening thought! Still, I suppose I should've had some clue. You hinted at certain things and indeed, some of your abilities back then didn't match who and what you portrayed yourself as.*::

If a granite statue could wear a look of chagrin, I certainly would've right then. ::*So much happened before I could tell you everything you needed to know.*:: She bristled as I spoke. ::*That's not an excuse. It's simply the way things worked out. I'd planned to tell you that weekend, when we were alone. Unfortunately, the attack on your family's mansion happened first.::*

My thoughts continued down that path, although I no longer actively projected them. I vividly remembered the complete chaos as the dark family, whose efforts they'd worked to undermine, attacked House Eventide.

::So much happened that night.:: Her emotional overtones carried nuances I couldn't readily identify.

::What do you mean?::

:: I learned I was pregnant immediately before the attack began.::

Her reply shook me to my core, for all that I'd discerned that she had to be the common denominator between Tawny and me. I sent her the mental equivalent of open arms and invited her to step into a long-overdue comforting embrace. She hesitated. *::I know there's a lot to clear up, but please, let me give you the hug you seem to need.::*

She accepted with a sigh that could've leveled mountains.

CHAPTER FOUR

After what felt like years but was really only moments later, Tatia spoke as she sank to the grass in front of my statue. ::*What happened that night?*::

::*Clarence Silvranus happened.*::

The look of shock on her face matched the sudden storm of emotion I felt from her.

"Is that..." Her words trailed off as she sat there trying to work through how that—or, rather, he—fit into the events of that fateful night. The fact that she forgot and spoke aloud was a measure of how off-balance the news threw her.

I completed her question. ::*The protégé of House Aphotic's head of family at the time? Yes. Except 'protégé' is misleading, because when Clarence tried to kill me, he said that the attack was his idea and plan.*::

Fresh shock reverberated across the link between us as she informed me, ::*Clarence is the current head of family and has been since Gabriel Silvranus was killed while attempting to force his way through the booby-trapped wards on our vault that night.*::

Oh, shit. That was not good news for anyone. Not even other dark families.

::*He's the biggest reason we've taught Tawny the dark spells, even though she's clearly a light being. She may well be the only one who can stop him when he strikes again. And he will strike. We're too much of a threat to his plans for him to leave us alone.::*

::His plans?::

::In a nutshell, he's trying to become Earth's sole warlord. He wants to control everything, not only magic.::

She sat there in silence as I processed all the unspoken information that accompanied her statement. There were so many layers and nuances that it would take far longer than one visit to work through everything. While I considered the ramifications of what she'd said, she had apparently thought along tangential lines.

::As well-sculpted a statue as you are...:: She snickered aloud before she mastered herself, and her amusement reached me through our link. *::Is it possible for you to regain your human form?::*

::I believe so, at least in some fashion.:: My mental tone turned as dry as the Sahara. *::The difficulty has been in executing the physical gestures needed to cast the spells correctly.::*

She slapped a hand over her mouth to contain her laughter and her eyes danced as her shoulders shook. A mental picture of a chimera trying to cast spells with its paws and tail reached me, and the image roared fire in frustration at its failure. She added speech bubbles to the picture, and little flames danced along the edges as she filled in some distinctly colorful language. Fresh laughter colored her thoughts since the chimera's language had a decidedly feminine slant—and Tatia knew I was as male as they came.

::Evil woman.:: My laughter joined hers as I responded with an image in which the chimera grabbed her with its tail, spun her around, and peppered her backside with tiny wisps of flame in retaliation.

::Uncle!:: Her mental image raised its hands in surrender, still giggling.

I huffed and sent back an image of the chimera stomping a

paw on the ground, then sobered. ::*We have much to talk about, and I suspect not much time to do it in. Where should we start?*::

She calmed as well and settled herself more comfortably on the grass. ::*The night of the attack. Things were total chaos. I saw you fighting against Gabriel Silvranus, and then was pulled away to help Sophie keep the younglings safe. When I made it back to where I'd last seen you, you were gone and Gabriel was dead.*::

I gathered my thoughts before speaking. ::*Soon after you left, Gabriel tried to force the wards. While he was casting, trying to unravel the booby traps, I did my best to interrupt him while battling Clarence. When it became clear that Gabriel wouldn't get through, Clarence upped his efforts to kill me and everyone else still in the House. I made myself a target to draw him away and protect as many as I could.*::

I paused as the remembered fear for those I'd cared for momentarily choked me. ::*He boasted during our fight that the attack was his idea. He'd come up with the battle plans as well but presented his ideas in such a way that Gabriel and his trusted council members thought they'd come up with them. What none of them realized was that Gabriel was meant to die.*::

Her horror at such cold-blooded machinations reverberated between us. ::*That's not all, is it?*::

::*No.*::

::*Tell me.*::

I steeled myself before admitting, ::*He damn near managed to kill me as well. I'm still not sure how I lived through the transfer into the chimera—the circumstances weren't exactly under control—but I know he fully expected me to die when he set the spell in motion.*::

Her emotions couldn't be hidden, although she kept her words concise. ::*How on earth did you counter that spell?*::

I started to reply but heard a quiet thought. ::*That asshole will pay for what he's done.*:: I assumed it was Tatia, but it was so quiet, I knew it wasn't intended to be heard.

As though I hadn't heard anything except Tatia's question, I continued. ::*I didn't counter it so much as twist it. It was a desperate gamble, one I wasn't sure would work. It took me a long time to realize I was alive, after a fashion, but melded with the statue. It took even longer before I realized I could feel things, and longer still to gain hearing and limited sight.::* I coughed before adding, somewhat tongue-in-cheek, *::Granite isn't the easiest thing to work with.::*

A brief flicker of amusement reached me. *::Sophie always said you were hard-headed at times but rock-solid when it came to what mattered.::*

::She would. Although I don't think she meant this.:: My answering humor died as quickly as it came.

Silence lay between us for a short time before Tatia broke it. *::You said you think you can regain your human form 'in some fashion.' What does that mean?::*

Leave it to her to go straight to the hard part. *::Since, presumably, my human body is deceased, think spirit-animated granite with an ability to walk, talk, feel, and shapeshift between chimera and human forms.::* I paused. *::Of course, there are parts of that logic that still need to be more fully researched and fine-tuned, but the principles behind the complex blend of spells to accomplish it seem sound.::*

She digested that in silence. I could feel her mind churn furiously as she thought. *::And if it doesn't work?::*

::Then I become granite in truth, not merely appearance.::

She rose to her feet and brushed stray blades of grass off her clothes before she faced me head-on.

::How do you plan to work around your inability to execute the physical components of the spells?::

::That's the million-dollar question.:: I left it at that.

CHAPTER FIVE

Several days passed after that conversation. I spent the time thinking after the germ of an idea made me delve deep into memories of my training.

It was a dreary day with rainclouds looming when Tatia next appeared. She unfolded a camp chair she'd brought and settled into it with a sigh, a Kindle held on her lap.

::*Rough day?*::

"Mother Nature, you can stop with the weather and pressure changes any time now. My bones ache." ::*Yes. Training, research, and this damn front coming through.*:: Her spoken thought overlaid her mental reply.

::*Ahh. I assume the first two are relevant to the discussion at hand.*::
::*They are.*::

Silence lay heavy between us for a moment before she broke it.

::*I've looked into transformation spells. Why don't you tell me what you've considered, and let's see if anything I found will help.*::

She settled back in her chair and swiped her finger across the Kindle's screen.

::*Why the sudden rush? And the assumption that I'll even try?*::

Her tangled mess of emotions—fear and grim determination predominant—hit me like a freight train to underscore her next words.

::Because we've learned that Clarence plans to attack and obliterate us—and everyone associated with our family—within the next ten days.::

Fuck. My. Life. My horror knew no bounds.

::My sentiments exactly,:: Tatia agreed.

I walked her through the combination of spells I'd settled on and she contributed some less-volatile alternatives. Now, we merely needed to determine how I could execute the gestures.

::There has to be a way, damn it!:: Her frustration was palpable.

Just then, Tawny burst around the corner of the hedge and almost ran into her grandmother's chair.

"Oh! Sorry, Gramma Tatia!"

Tatia chuckled softly. "Perhaps slowing down when rounding hedge corners is in order." It was the mildest of rebukes, delivered in a droll tone, but her meaning was clear.

Tawny nodded. *::I'm not interrupting, am I?::* Her thought was directed to both of us.

::A short break won't hurt.::

::Oh, good. May I climb up?::

Her request caught me off guard. *::Er, okay...::*

"Child, what—" Tatia suddenly stopped speaking and watched intently as Tawny swarmed up my base and foreleg and half-vaulted, half-levitated onto my back. Once she was seated astride me, she leaned against my neck and wrapped her arms around it.

::Thank you.:: Tawny's mental gratitude warmed me as much as her physical warmth slowly heated the granite beneath her. Then, almost too soft to be heard, *::I only wish I knew why I felt so safe around you—like nothing bad can happen.::*

::*Tatia, does she know?*::

::*She does not.*:: Her reply was instant.

Long moments passed before Tatia spoke to me again. ::*What if the three of us linked to cast the spells? Tawny is powerful but untried at that level of complexity. I can handle the complexity but risk not being strong enough to weave and maintain that many spells at once. You're both powerful and capable but can't execute the gestures. But if we linked...*::

I ran through all the logic trees as fast as my brain could think. ::*Yes... It could work, but... You realize that if things go wrong, they'll probably be disastrous.*::

::*I know.*::

::*There's something you're not telling me. What is it?*::

She took a deep, shuddering breath. ::*We—meaning Tawny, Sophie, myself, and the rest of House Eventide—probably won't prevail without your help. I'd rather risk possible disaster than not try it and face certain obliteration.*::

Put like that, the choice was simple. ::*Very well. Do you want to ask her or shall I?*::

::*I'll do it.*:: She paused. ::*Do we tell her who you are now, or later?*::

::*Later. Assuming it works—and we survive.*::

CHAPTER SIX

I could dimly sense Tatia and Tawny communicating, although since they hadn't included me in their discussion, I didn't know what was said. I knew when Tatia asked her about being part of the spellcasting link, though. Tawny stiffened in shock and almost slipped off me as she shot upright from leaning against my neck. She recovered with the help of a quick levitation spell.

::*You want me to* what?:: Her words rang in my head. Judging by Tatia's wince, she had the same experience.

::*Let me*,:: I shot privately to Tatia. ::*Tawny, how much of the situation has Tatia shared with you?*::

::*Most of it, I think.*::

::*So you know your House is facing—*::

::*Obliteration?*:: she interrupted. ::*Yes. She also said that if we link together, we can cast spells that will help you transform.*::

::*Did she explain why she wants to do this and why the three of us together have a real chance to successfully pull off some very complex spells?*::

::*I interrupted her before she got that far.*:: Tawny's sheepish reply was matched by her emotions.

I heard Tatia's audible snort, although she otherwise stayed quiet.

::Tawny, the first 'why' is because without my help, your House is likely to fall. None of us want that. The second 'why' is because the three of us are already linked, so forming a deeper link to cast spells is merely an extension of what we already have and use.::

Tatia snorted again at my use of the word "merely" but didn't call me out, which I appreciated. As strong and precocious as Tawny was, she was still a young teenager. She needed to be confident in her abilities if we wanted to pull this off.

::When will we do this?:: Tawny asked.

Tatia sent me a wordless query.

I steeled myself. *::No time like the present.::*

Tatia directed Tawny to stay where she was and explained that the physical connection was as important as the mental and emotional ones. While she spoke, she stood, folded her chair, and stashed it out of sight. When she returned, she stood with one foot touching my base but left herself enough room for the hand and arm gestures she'd need to make while casting. *::Ready?::*

::Ready, Gramma Tatia.::

::Let us begin.:: I spoke formally to set the tone and intention we needed to direct the magic.

The time that followed was interminable. The effort required to maintain such a deep link and channel power through it threatened to tear us apart more than once. Tawny became our bedrock. She anchored us when the flow of power and increasing complexity of our spells tried to cast us adrift.

Tatia glowed and the spells manifested as a golden nimbus that grew brighter and more opaque as we continued.

The spot where Tawny sat astride me grew ever warmer and radiated deeper into the stone than even the most searing rays of sun ever reached.

Finally, as Tatia completed the last gestures and brought the chant to a shouted crescendo, I yelled to Tawny, ::*Off!*:: I pictured her joining Tatia on the ground and both of them pressing their hands and bodies against the base of my statue to channel the golden cloud onto me.

Tawny had other ideas.

::*Gramma Tatia!*:: Her shout deafened us as she indicated for Tatia to feed it *through* her like a conduit. All that careened between us faster than the blink of an eye—far faster than I had time to naysay it.

Tatia realized at once what Tawny had intuited and channeled the energy-filled golden haze into her in a steady stream. Tawny sent it into me in turn and let it radiate from her entire body. She gave the last laggard tendrils a little boost to push them to flow through.

The effect of so much energy channeled into my granite shell started a chain reaction deep inside. The first outward sign was when the statue started to shake. Tawny, still connected to me mentally but with an outside vantage point, was the first to realize that the flashpoint approached. She launched herself off me, grabbed Tatia, and ran for cover.

Pain! My world became nothing but pain as my mind, soul, and memories of being human melded fully with the granite chimera and morphed slowly into a cohesive whole. Unmoving granite became something…other. I wasn't sure how to describe it. All I knew was that, agonizingly slowly, I gained the ability to move.

My tail twitched and leg muscles quivered. In almost the same moment, my whiskers came to life and reported things that sight, sound, and smell couldn't discern. My ears swiveled. One paw lifted free and cracked the granite base. Shivers ran up my back and my tail whipped from side to side. After a stomp with a different paw, more cracks appeared in the base.

Almost there floated through my mind as more of my body came alive. My sides heaved as I drew in great breaths of air. With a few more paw stomps, all four were now free. My heads swiveled to either side and I flung them up as I roared. *Free!*

I leaped off the granite and stumbled as I landed on the grass. Four paws didn't work anywhere near the same as two legs—a fact I needed to remember in order to fight effectively. Which, judging by the alarm that shrilled across my senses just then, looked more like "when" rather than "if."

"Sonofabitch!" Tatia's uncharacteristic swearing as she felt the alarm was enough for me to race around the hedge toward them. My senses had easily pinpointed their location.

"Andar, I hope you're ready—because it looks like we ran out of time."

CHAPTER SEVEN

As much as I wanted to see if I could morph into human form, I needed to adjust to this one first. Plus, I needed to save my energy for the battle.

I met with Tatia and Tawny a few hundred feet further on, my gait considerably smoother now. Fire roiled in my chest. It was an odd sensation. *::Where is he? Can you pinpoint him?::* I stayed with mind-speech since it gave us an advantage.

Tatia caught on. *::He tripped the perimeter alarm at the outer edge of the formal garden. When he moves closer, different patterns will warn us of distance and location.::* She paused. *::Tawny—::*

::Stays with us,:: I interrupted firmly. *::The three of us need to stay together, because it'll take all three of us working in concert to defeat him.::* I'd let my physical and magical senses range out as we moved. The information they returned wasn't good: Clarence had become significantly stronger over the years.

The stone on Tatia's necklace—an amulet, I realized—flashed three times in quick succession, then subsided. *::Sophie and the youngsters are safe. For now.::* That last was added rather grimly, since they were safe only as long as there were defenders to shield them.

Another alarm shrilled across our skin, followed closely by a third in a different pattern. *::Clarence is headed this way. His minions are moving through the formal garden toward the mansion.::* Tatia's amulet flashed again—four times, each flash a second apart. *::Good. Defenses are active, and defenders are all in place.::* A quick double flash. *::Allies have arrived as well!::* An overwhelming sense of relief flooded across our link.

::Then let's bait this asshole to a spot of our choosing and end this once and for all.:: I bounded ahead, a particular spot already in mind.

::Where—Oh!:: Tatia absorbed the image of the weathered gold gyroscope globe from my thoughts.

Tawny did as well and added, *::I know a shortcut!::*

She cut through an opening on our right. It was barely wide enough for me to squeeze through, although each branch in the opening tried to take its pound of flesh out of me. *Score one for animated granite,* I thought irreverently. I heard Tawny snicker from her spot in the lead. Whoops. I hadn't meant to broadcast that. Oh well...a little humor before battle wasn't necessarily a bad thing.

We reached the gyroscope after several minutes of zigzagging our way through the maze. Tawny took shortcuts whenever possible. We staggered to a stop on the grass and tried to catch our breath. So far, there was no sign of Clarence, which suited my plans perfectly.

::Why here?:: Tawny finally asked.

::The gyroscope,:: I replied.

::Wait... You mean to use it somehow? Is that even possible?::

::Yes. The outer coating on the rings and globe is gold, which is an excellent conductor for magic. The globe can be used as temporary storage for a single spell. It's extremely unorthodox but will work for a limited time. The rings will spin according to the forces directed upon them. If we play our cards right, we can slingshot the stored spell from multiple directions simultaneously. It's a one-shot deal, though,

because once Clarence figures out what we're doing, he'll use it against us.::

::Got it.::

::Andar, which spell do you have in mind?::

::I have two possibilities, Tatia. Do you have an idea?::

::No, but I think Tawny does.::

::Tawny? What's your idea?::

::Phantom blade slice. Also known as 'death by a thousand cuts.'::
The image she sent was chilling. I could feel her extreme dislike for the spell, but she was correct that it had the best chance to eliminate Clarence—or, at least, incapacitate him long enough to finish him by other means.

::Tatia?:: I sought her confirmation.

::I agree.:: Her next thought was for me alone. ::This is the spell Sophie taught her, and this situation is why. Somehow—and I've no idea how—Sophie knew it would happen like this.::

::Let's do it, then. Tawny, you know the spell. Go ahead and cast it. Tatia and I will back you and help you set it for a triggered release. I'll handle the bait. Tatia, let me know when Clarence crosses the wards closest to here.::

Tawny closed her eyes and set to work. Her lips moved as she silently spoke the words to the spell. With fluid hand gestures, she traced shapes and sigils in the air with a yew wood wand I hadn't seen her use before. Several of the sigils glowed as she worked, leaving afterimages behind as she sent them to overlay the rings and globe. She circled the gyroscope steadily as she worked and never once stumbled although her eyes remained closed.

Tatia worked some complicated spells while she monitored both the wards and Tawny. A quick scrutiny of the pattern she traced with her alder wood wand showed me the delayed-trigger trap spell she placed on the ground. I noticed she'd been careful to weave us and any members of House Eventide in as exceptions to the trigger.

A wordless nudge from Tawny brought my attention back to her. She was ready to set her trigger and sink the spell into the globe and rings. I passed her the images of what that looked like and coached her through the process. She followed each step flawlessly. The spell settled into place, glowed faintly as the last layers came to rest, then faded until it became invisible.

Tatia spoke. ::*He's crossing the patio wards. There's only one more between there and here.*::

She finished her trap spell and looked at Tawny and me. ::*Good work. I have a few other surprises waiting as well. Andar, what did you have in mind as bait?*::

::*This.*:: I lifted the cloaking spell I'd had over the area while they worked and made it seem like it was raggedly coming apart as they tried to hide.

::*He's crossing the final ward.*:: Tatia's tension showed. ::*He's at the hedge...* Shield!*:: she shouted as all three of us felt Clarence's assault.

He walked through the opening and onto the grass in front of us.

"Well, well, well. If it isn't my lucky day, finding the two of you here together. Thank you for making it easy to take you both out at once." He looked at me. "A chimera? Tsk, tsk...what *have* the two of you been playing with?" He shook his head in mock affront even as he launched multiple attacks on Tatia and Tawny.

They ducked and dodged to avoid as many of the physical attacks as possible while countering the more dangerous attempts with spells of their own. The battle quickly grew heated, with a vicious crossfire of spells that rebounded off the gyroscope. Fortunately, nothing tripped our dormant spell. As the combat progressed, Clarence turned far enough during his relentless attacks on Tatia and Tawny that I was now behind him.

I took advantage of that to flame his back and used magic to cast a cone of silence over the stream of fire that roared from me. Additional magic separated it into dozens of smaller tongues that licked at him from every possible direction. I wanted him to think the women generated the attack, not me. I maintained the assault on his shields as I tried to weaken them and create holes where other attacks could penetrate.

Finally, it happened. He shifted enough of his weakening shields to the front that a small opening appeared in the center of his back. *::Tawny! Now!::* I shouted, as my thoughts flashed to her triggering the phantom blade slice spell.

The already-spinning gyroscope settled into a steady pattern and the spell activated. I threw up a hasty shield and angled it in front of me so the outer edges of the attack were funneled toward Clarence. He stiffened as the first blades pierced his shields and sliced his flesh. Ribbons of red erupted on his back and upper legs. He began to cast new shielding spells and I released another blast of fire at him. The blaze destroyed his wand and crisped the flesh on his hands before he could complete his defenses.

He rallied grimly and used an incantation designed to paralyze any living being within the spell's radius. Tawny threw up a mirror-shield and hauled Tatia and me into a link. Her lightning-quick thoughts directed us to form it into a sphere around Clarence and the still-spinning gyroscope.

::Hold...hold until the spells have finished him.:: The girl's voice was laden with horror and guilt at what we were doing but was nonetheless resolute. *::He must not be allowed to live.::*

Her voice sounded different as she delivered that last implacable judgement. Tatia stiffened. I felt her shock through the link. *::Tawny?::*

::Tawny has agreed to let me see and speak through her for the time it takes for Clarence Silvranus' final judgement to be rendered. She will not be harmed. I've given my oath.::

Tatia relaxed minutely.

Clearly, this was a turn of events she hadn't expected, but now was *not* the time to ask what was going on.

Hard on the heels of that thought, the mirror-shield imploded with a small *pop* to reveal a bloody, human-shaped shredded form.

::Judgement has been rendered and the sentence carried out. Clarence Silvranus no longer exists.::

The disembodied voice rang through the heads of everyone on the premises. Several members of his House who were still fighting dropped where they stood. All life left them between one breath and the next as they met the same fate. The voice vanished in the same moment.

Tawny shook herself, her eyes shadowed by the burden of taking a life but remarkably clear of all further guilt. I suspected that whoever had used her eyes and voice had a hand in that.

Tatia sank to the ground near her, exhausted. I walked over to both of them and sat behind Tatia, inviting her to use me as a backrest. Tawny plopped down and did the same. Soon after, Sophie raced across the grass and fell to her knees in front of us to draw Tawny and Tatia into a hug.

"He's gone," I heard her whisper raggedly through her sobs as she held them. "He's finally gone."

FINIS

AUTHOR NOTES

Cast in Stone turned into wild ride spawned by a brainstorming post in the Oriceran Fans Write for Fans Facebook group. I commented an idea, Paul flipped it around, we all went *"oooh!"*— and there it sat. I didn't intend to use it. I'd thrown it out there for others. <<laughs>> Yep, famous last words. Months later, the start of this story sprang into mind and continued writing itself before I was even fully awake, screaming at me until I finally got it jotted down—mostly coherently—in a note on my phone. Thus began the tale of how one short story upstaged another—one I already had two-thirds written.

Huge thanks to Martha Carr, Michael Anderle, and all the talented authors who brought this universe to brilliant life, helped it grow—then opened the gates to let others add to the magic.

I hope you enjoyed meeting Tawny, Andar, and Tatia. Reader feedback is always welcome. Feel free to drop me an email at tbyrnesauthor(at)gmail(dot)com or connect with me in the Oriceran Fans or Oriceran Fans Write groups on Facebook. Other published work is listed on my Amazon author page, https://www.amazon.com/Tracey-Byrnes/e/B07DHXCDWS.

AUTHOR NOTES

Magia est aeternum.
Tracey Byrnes

UNEXPECTED DISCOVERY

BY T.L. GRYFEN

A trip to say goodbye literally ends with Teri falling into another world. Now, can she find what she's been searching for?

When Teri's fiancé vanished on the night of their anniversary, her life changed in an instant. In a split second, she lost her future and her sanity. On a trip to their favorite place, in an attempt to say goodbye and reclaim her life, she accidentally crashes through a portal and into another world.

Will this accidental trip lead to an unexpected outcome?

DEDICATION

Dedicated to my ex-boyfriend Mark Franceschini. After eight years of not knowing what happened, I finally got my closure. I know you are finally working at your dream, and now, so am I. Thank you for the time we had, and good luck with your future.
I would also like to dedicate this to my mom, who as always, cheers me on to greater and greater attempts at writing.

UNEXPECTED DISCOVERY

Teri sat on the tree stump at Clingman's Dome and stared blindly out over the view of the Appalachians. She had decided to drive up to the park on a whim and had hoped that perhaps visiting this place, on this date, would finally bring her some peace. So far, all it had done was make her mourn her loss out loud.

"How long is long enough to grieve? How long will this hole in my center last? It's been eight fucking years, and I still can't get thoughts of you out of my head. It would be different if I had any idea of where you were or what the hell happened. How did you completely disappear in this age of technology? When everyone tweets about their pets, puts their lunches on Instagram, and spills their life stories online, how does a forty-year-old man simply vanish? Your family hasn't heard from you and nor has your job. You went out to run a few errands before dinner and then, you were gone.

"The police found your car in the parking lot at the grocery store. The guy at ABC said he remembered seeing you when you bought a bottle of Godiva liqueur, told him it was for our anniversary, and left. The waitress at the Mexican restaurant on the corner said she saw you start toward the car and then look at the woods like someone had called your name. The police searched there, though. They found some weird dirt and plants, but nothing to show there was a struggle, so you weren't kidnapped.

"They closed the case last year and said you had been gone long enough to be declared dead. I know you aren't dead. I can *feel* that you aren't dead. You're merely gone. So, I came here. You once spun me a story about magic right here in this spot. You said that you had something to tell me, but before you did, you wanted to tell me a story about another universe where witches, elves, and vampires lived. Where people with wings flew around and flowers danced. You spun a tale of worlds crossing over, of denizens of another world settling in this one. You told me that this place was somewhere that the magic and wonder leaked through into our world. Then, you kissed me, and that was all the wonder and magic I ever needed."

She stood and brushed herself off and continued to stare out over the valley as tears poured silently down here face. "I miss you, Marc. I know you didn't leave me deliberately. I have to believe that something took you away from me against your will. But...I have to move on. My friends and family are worried about me and even your family is worried about me. So, I will take a last hike in this magical place you loved and then I'll say goodbye. I will always love you, but I can't keep hoping you'll come back from wherever it is you've gone. Hopefully, I'll find some magic here that will make me miss you a little less."

Teri turned, passed the countless cars in the park's overfilled parking lot, and headed toward the trail down the side of the mountain.

As she hiked, she tried to take joy in the little things along her path like watching the birds and squirrels in the trees around her. She inhaled deeply, savored the spicy scent of autumn, and tried once again to identify what plant produced the elusive smell of vanilla and corn that seemed to permeate the air. A memory brought a smile. Marc had always laughed at her description of the smell and could never single it out from the air the way she could. Lost in her thoughts, she reached a barely visible path that followed alongside the stream and turned down it. Finally soothed by the forest, she continued and only paid enough attention to where she walked to avoid tripping over rocks in the trail. After an hour or so, she heard a muted roar, and the air became more humid.

A sense of excitement welled in her stomach and chest and Teri rushed heedlessly down the path. She thrust through a scrubby break between the brilliantly colored trees and into a wide clearing. A waterfall plunged over rocks and thundered into a deep lake. Curious, she wandered closer. As she approached, the foliage greened and the air became warmer. Enchanted by the lushness and a little weary from the exertion, Teri ignored the strangeness of her surroundings and sat at the edge of the pool to rest. Lured by the steam rising from the surface, she pulled off her hiking boots and thick socks and put her feet in the hot water. After a few moments in which she sat and absorbed the warmth, she noticed other muscles had begun to ache. Without thought, she stripped her clothes off and submerged her whole body.

When she surfaced, she released a choking sob and broke down. All the sadness she had hoarded for the last eight years poured from her in a torrent.

"Marc, I don't know how to do this. I live my life on autopilot. I don't know what happened to you, so I can't move on. I'm afraid to let myself get involved with anyone else because I'm afraid they will leave me too. " She laughed. "Hell, you vanishing did wonders for my abandonment issues, let me tell you." Unable to stop herself, she spewed her emotions—screamed, cried, lectured, and even laughed. She poured it all into the roar of the waterfall, and when she was done, let herself fall limply back to float and stare at the sky.

As the shadows deepened over the pool, Teri felt her drifting thoughts begin to clear. Abruptly, she bolted upright. Now that her clouded thoughts had focused, it occurred to her how strange her surroundings were. It was November in the Smoky Mountains, so why were all the trees and the grass green? Where in the world had a hot spring with a forty-foot waterfall come from? Deciding to investigate, she paddled to the edge and waded out of the water. Using her sweater as a towel, she dried off and got dressed, leaving her sweater spread out on a bush to dry with her belt pack hidden under it.

Ignoring the lush forest, she decided to focus on the area of the waterfall, hoping that perhaps there, she would find some clue as to where exactly this place was. Slowly, she approached the cascading water and peered at the ground and along the shore of the small lake. Closer to the waterfall itself, she noticed footprints, but whether due to the fading light or the blurriness of her tear-strained eyes, she could not distinguish them clearly enough for identification. Teri rubbed her eyes and shook her head.

The tracks were small like a child's, but the tips were clearly clawed. She chose to ignore the oddness of the footprints themselves, followed them, and eventually reached a slender protrusion of naked rock that stretched through a narrow gap into an open area behind the falls. Realizing that there was no way she would be able to get behind the falls on that path without getting soaked, she backtracked along the shore. She needed to find a way to cross the lake and possibly find a drier route in from there.

Suddenly, a rustling from the woods caught her attention. Startled, Teri looked around for a hiding place. With no suitable cover, she backed slowly away from the area the sound came from. Praying that whoever—or whatever—was about to emerge from the underbrush wouldn't see her, she knelt silently and watched. After a few minutes of increased activity and muffled curses, two small figures emerged from the woods, arguing with one another. As they stepped into the fading light, she suppressed a gasp. They looked like large rats wearing clothes.

"What the hell was in that water?" she muttered to herself. "I'm seeing bipedal rats dressed in Renny garb. I have to be hallucinating." She glanced back at the lake and then at the green grass and trees surrounding her. "I must have fallen on the path and hit my head. I am obviously laying on the hiking trail somewhere dying, and this place is what my brain came up with to entertain me while it happens."

She blinked a few times and looked up again. The two figures were still there. "Seriously, giant rats? What's next? Four turtles and a pizza? No, this is stupid. I am not seeing this. I'll close my eyes, and when I open them, the giant rats will be gone." Still muttering to herself, Teri closed her eyes and kept them shut for a few minutes. When she opened them again, the two figures were no longer visible, and she sighed in relief. "I was right. I only imagined it."

"Who are you talking to, love?"

"What?" Teri jumped and looked behind her. One of the rats stood and stared at her. "What the hell are you? Rats don't talk!"

"It's a good thing I'm not a rat then, isn't it? My name is Sean. I'm a Willen, not a rat."

"A Willen? You mean Marc didn't make stories up? There are witches, and vampires, and winged people who all live on another planet?"

"Yep, pretty much."

"You really exist and I haven't gone crazy? There really is a magical world linked to mine, filled with magical creatures?"

"Well, I don't know if you are crazy or not, but the rest of that is true."

"What are you doing here? Marc told me that Willens lived on Oriceran, not on Earth. Why would you be in North Carolina?"

"I live in North Carolina, in the kemana under Clingman's Dome. My whole family does. Before that, we lived in London. And I should ask you what you're doing here. Because we are *not* in North Carolina, love, and while humans do live in Oriceran, it's not anywhere near there."

"What do you mean? Of course we're in North Carolina. I walked down from the park. I couldn't be in Oriceran. How would I possibly get here?" Teri shivered involuntarily. "I've gone nuts. I'm talking to a figment of my imagination. I can't be in in Oriceran because there is no Oriceran. It's merely a story Marc made up during our date. I'm delusional."

"You are not delusional! How many times do I have to tell you that? As for how you got here, you said you walked down from the park, right? I think I know how you wound up here. I paid a witch to open a portal so I could bring some stuff over to the black market. You must have crossed over while it was still open."

"The black market? Oh, that's right. Marc said Willen were thieves—" She stopped for a second and shook her head. "What am I doing? I keep talking to a figment of my imagination. Ouch!" She clutched her arm where the Willen had pinched her. "What was that for?"

"So that you would stop saying I'm imaginary. You'll give me a complex. Look, lady, I don't know who this Marc guy was, or how he knew about Oriceran or it's natives. But you are not imagining me, and you aren't delusional. Oriceran does exist, so do Willens, and witches and vampires and everything else this guy told you about. He was also right about Willens being...rather acquisitional. I think my acquaintance stole your sweater, sorry. Look, the portal has closed, so you won't get back to Earth tonight. Let me take you into town. I know someone there who can give you a place to stay."

"I don't know if I should follow strange creatures into the

woods." Teri laughed when she realized the absurdity of the statement even as she said it.

Sean raised an eyebrow at her, something that made her laugh even more. "Would you rather sleep in the woods? There are all sorts of creatures that would simply love to make a dinner of you. I feel responsible because you wound up here because of my business venture, but it's your decision. I have places to be, and it's supper time."

She looked around the clearing at the forest that now seemed to crowd in. The once idyllic looking setting began to look ominous as the light faded. The roar of the waterfall no longer sounded soothing but discordant. Added to that, her stomach growled demandingly.

"Okay. You're right. If this really is another world, I know nothing about it, or its dangers. I would be grateful if you could help me find somewhere safe to stay. Just to let you know, though, I don't have a way to pay for anything—at least, I don't think I do. You don't take Earth money, do you?"

"Actually, depending on what you have, somebody might take it. But you won't need to pay for this. I have a friend in the area, and she'll give you a bed for the night and some dinner. I'll see what I can do about getting you back to North Carolina tomorrow. Is there anyone who will miss you if you aren't home tonight?"

"No, not tonight. My mom knows I will be out of town for a day or two, and my cat has plenty of food and water." Teri looked around. "I can't believe all the stories Marc told me were true. How did he know? How could he have possibly known that there was a whole other world? How did he know about the—what did you call it, kemana?—under Clingman's Dome?"

She stood from where she had knelt on the ground and turned to Sean. "If this is all real—if you are real—where are the dancing flowers he talked about? Why don't you act like a Willen?"

"I don't know how your friend knew about Oriceran. Maybe he was magical, or maybe he knew someone who was. That particular breed of flower doesn't grow around here, but deeper into the woods, they are all over the place. As for me, I wasn't raised by Willen. I was an orphan raised by a witch and an elf. They took in a whole bunch of us magical kids who were left orphaned by Rhazdon's followers. Because I was raised by slightly more human-like people, I don't really have the typical Willen personality. Although I do like to 'borrow' things from people, and I make a killing smuggling from Oriceran to Earth and back again."

Sean offered Teri his arm. "Come on, let's get you settled with my friend, Niana. She's a good person—a witch. She used to live on Earth, and she'd love to hear all about what is going on there now. But don't tell anyone except her where you are from. Portal travel is illegal, and you don't want to get arrested."

Teri gave him her arm and smiled. "Don't worry about me. I still feel like I'm in a walking dream. I won't talk to anyone about being from another world. If this really is Oriceran, I'll get arrested. If it's not, I'll be put in a psych ward, so either way, I'm locked up. No thanks. I'm claustrophobic and couldn't take that. Just show me to food and a bed, please."

He led her past the waterfall and into the woods but steered her away from the narrow path that led behind it. "We don't want to go that way, love. It leads to a cave filled with contraband. Lots of wealth, but no warmth or food." He smiled at her and the expression looked strange on his face. "Niana should have supper ready soon. Town is about a mile away. If we hurry, we can hopefully make it before full dark. Let's go."

They walked arm and arm and Teri leaned down a little to accommodate the shorter Willen as they hurried along a path that appeared in the woods before them. Soon, they left the clearing and waterfall behind.

After about twenty minutes at a steady pace, as the sun dropped behind the trees in what she assumed was still the west, a small town came into view. To Teri, it strongly resembled an educational historic village, such as the one she had visited with her family at the Foxfire museum in Georgia. The scent of the evening meal cooking permeated the air and signs of a living village were visible in the worn ruts in the road and the shops that stood with their doors open, inviting late customers to come in and shop. Sean released her arm and led the way through the center of the village to a slightly larger home on the far edge of town, where he paused.

"Okay, this is Niana's house. Let me go in and let her know who you are and why you are here. She's a friendly lady, but she isn't fond of uninvited strangers. Once she knows who you are, though, and that it's my fault you are stuck here for now, she'll be happy to have you visit with her. Wait here. I'll be right back."

Teri nodded in agreement and studied what she could see of the town from where she stood. Directly in her line of sight was a building that, even to her unaccustomed eye, looked like a bar or pub. Sounds of laughter and music drifted from it, along with the unmistakable smell of beer. She barely noticed Sean's absence as her attention was immediately caught by the flowers in the flower box. The brightly colored plants seemed to dance and sway to the music and moved on their own, with no wind stirring them. She took a moment to marvel that all this was real.

As inconceivable as it was, she was really in a land where flowers danced and rats—Willens, she corrected herself—walked upright and talked. It was overwhelming, and she hoped that when she woke in the morning, it would still all be true. She didn't want to consider the possibility that she might be lying in a hospital bed somewhere—or worse, injured on a trail and lost in the Great Smokies Park. As the door opened behind her, she took a breath of the exotically scented air overlaid with the familiar smells of beer and food, determined to enjoy this whole experience. She had already seen things she would have never believed possible, and now, she would meet a witch. She turned to face Sean who stood in the doorway and raised an eyebrow.

"So, have you prepared your friend for me? I wouldn't want her to cast a spell on me when I walk in." She laughed.

"She won't cast any spells. I told Niana all about you—well as much as I know about you, at least—and about what happened. She's looking forward to meeting you. I warn you, she has all sorts of questions about what has happened on your world for the last eight years. That's the last time she had any real news. Those of us who live in the kemana don't usually pay attention to human world gossip. Come on, she's anxious to meet you." He held his arm out and waited for her to put her hand on it, then led the way into the house.

As she walked into the witch's house with Sean, Teri looked around, curious. She halfway expected it to look like something from a Disney or horror movie and was almost disappointed at how normal it looked. More of the dancing flowers grew in pots on small tables everywhere she looked, and books were stacked on every flat surface. She smiled and made a note to ask her hostess if she could borrow a book. Sean led her through a comfortable living room, past an overstuffed flowered couch, and into a small homey kitchen. As they entered, he called out to the amethyst-haired woman who stood at the stove.

"Niana, as promised, this is Teri. I imagine she's starving by now. I know she didn't have any food with her when I found her, and that was a good while ago. Even if she isn't hungry, I know I'm starving. Do you think we could have something to eat? It smells great in here."

The woman called over her shoulder, "Come wash your hands, Sean, and make sure you don't shed in my kitchen. I won't sweep up piles of Willen hair." She turned the water in her sink off and reached for a towel. "I'll be right with you both. I have few things to finish up. Sean, you know where everything is. Get our guest something to drink. There's a fresh pitcher of juice in the cold pantry. Teri, go ahead and have a seat. You must be exhausted."

"Thank you. You have a lovely house. Very warm and inviting."

"It's not what you were expecting, is it?"

"Honestly, no. It's a little too...normal. After all the stories I've heard about witches, I expected something a little more, uh, occult." She took the glass of juice that Sean handed her and sat at the small table already set with three place settings. "Not that it isn't a beautiful house, what I have seen of it at least. I love it, honestly. All it needs is a giant bath tub to be perfect." She looked down as she spoke and fought to keep her eyes open.

"That's what I've always said." As she spoke, Niana turned to the table and placed a pot of stew in the center. "Why don't you help yourself to stew while I get the bread from the oven?" Teri looked hungrily at the food and reached for the serving spoon. Then, remembering her manners, she glanced at her hostess to thank her. When she had a good look at Niana's face, though, she gasped and paled in shock. She dropped the glass of juice and the crash echoed in the sudden silence as she jumped back and knocked her chair over.

"What the hell? Nina? You're Nina, Marc's sister. He had a picture of you in his wallet. You were a lot younger and definitely did *not* have purple hair in that photo. What the fuck is going on here? How are you even on Oriceran? Have you seen Marc? Is he okay? He disappeared from the grocery store parking lot eight years ago!"

Teri continued to babble as Niana stared her in shock. "How

can you be here and your parents be in Charlotte? Are they even really your parents?" Teri trembled, finally overcome by the stresses of the day. Shock at her many discoveries as well as exhaustion and hunger combined to overwhelm her, and her vision narrowed quickly. Niana's appalled face was the last thing she saw as the world faded to black.

When Teri regained consciousness, she lay on the soft couch, covered with a lavender-scented blanket. For a moment, she allowed herself to relax into the embrace of the upholstery, unwilling to open her eyes and return to her current confusing reality. Unrealistically, she half hoped that when she finally opened her eyes, she would be on her mother's couch napping and not in some strange person's living room on another planet. She dreaded having to face Nina—Niana, she reminded herself—and Sean after she'd passed out in the kitchen. She honestly wasn't sure that she could take any more surprises. Reluctantly, she stretched and opened her eyes. Sean and Niana sat in chairs facing the couch, waiting for her. When she stirred, the witch leaned forward with a concerned look.

"Teri, are you okay? You fell hard and Sean tried to catch you, but...well he's about seven inches shorter than you are, so it didn't work really well."

"Yeah, I'm fine. I just...I'd had enough. I couldn't take one more shock. Thank you for putting me on the couch and I'm so sorry I passed out. I thought you were somebody else, somebody you couldn't possibly be. I can't apologize enough."

"No, Teri, I need to apologize. I think I might be exactly who you thought I was. I do have an older brother—or I did. He was born first, although we were actually twins. I lost track of him years ago. My family lived in the kemana under Clingman's Dome until the two of us turned eighteen. I met a smuggler, fell in love, thought I was grown up, and followed him here to Oriceran. My parents moved, and my brother decided to try living in the human world. I've only seen him once since then. What about this Marc you were talking about? Who was he to you?"

"Marc was my fiancé. He had a picture that looked exactly like you in his wallet. When I asked, he said it was his little sister, Nina. He and I were about to celebrate the third anniversary of our first date when he simply disappeared. He left to run errands and never came home. The local police found his car in a parking lot. The clerk from the liquor store said he saw him walk into the woods on the side of the parking lot, and he never returned. Nobody has seen him in eight years. Exactly eight years today, as a matter of fact."

"Do you have a picture of your fiancé?"

"Yes, of course I do. Here..." She went to reach into her pack, then realized it wasn't on her. "Uhm, Sean, have you seen my belt pack? I don't remember if I picked it up at the falls."

Sean jumped. "Uhm, yes...actually, I did find it at the falls before I came to talk to you." He looked embarrassed. "I intended to give it back, I promise. Here."

He handed it to Teri, and she unzipped it and dug around for a minute before she exclaimed in triumph, "This is a picture of him taken about a month before he vanished."

Niana took the picture with a murmured thanks and stared at it for a moment. "This is him. This is Einmarco, my twin. You call him Marc? I see he dyed his hair to better fit in as human. It was always a deep shade of indigo before—the same shade as his eyes, actually. The raven-black suits him and I guess if the indigo showed through, he could blame it on the way the light reflects. You said you were engaged to him?"

"Yes. We had been engaged for six months when he disappeared. We were supposed to get married that May at Clingman's

Dome—I guess at the kemana, really. You said you saw him again after you moved here. When was that?"

"Probably about eight years ago, a few months after you say he disappeared. He seemed distracted and disoriented. He said something about having to get back to Earth, but he wouldn't tell me why. He stayed with me for a day or so. Then, when I woke up one morning, he was gone. I know he was trying to find someone to portal him back, but he didn't know anyone here anymore."

"How did he even get here, though, Niana? He wasn't anywhere near Clingman's Dome, and the guy who saw him said he looked like somebody had called his name."

"I don't know. He never said how he got to Oriceran. It wouldn't have had to be near a kemana, though. Anyone who has strong enough magic and knows how can open a portal, but it's illegal. All someone had to do was open a portal and call out to him. My question is why? And why has he not made it back to you yet? I can't imagine him staying away this long. Something has to have happened to him. We have to find him."

Teri looked at Niana with tears in her eyes. "Tell me the truth. Do you think he is alive? Or do you think he died trying to get back to me? Or did he maybe change his mind and decide to stay here? Maybe he didn't really love me as much as he said he did."

"No. If he said he loved you, then he did. My brother would never have lied about that. He believed—no, believes—in soul mates. And I can't believe that he is dead. He's my twin. I would know. Teri, please let me help you find him? Now that I know that he never made it home, I won't be able to do anything but worry. Plus, you could use someone who knows magic."

"Of course I want you to help me. We have to find him fast, though. It's already been eight years and I have this fear that we will find him too late."

"Well, now that I know he is missing and not back on Earth, I can help you find him. We should have an answer fairly quickly.

There really are only a few possibilities. He was captured and sent to prison, he encountered a trap or something, or he is dead. I refuse to believe he is dead, so it has to be one of the other two."

Still holding back her tears, Teri smiled wetly. "So where do we start, Niana? From what I know, Oriceran is a whole planet, so how do we start looking for one man in all that? It seems overwhelming."

The witch smiled. "That's the easy part. We use magic. Usually, I would need something of his to trace him with, but I'm his twin—his blood—so we don't need anything else. Now, this particular spell is technically considered blood magic, so it is frowned upon by the authorities. But..." Here, Niana grinned. "I have never been a rule-follower." She continued. "We should be fine. It will take me a day to get all the materials I need for my spell, and we need to decide what we will do when we have a direction to look in."

Teri smiled softly, "Then we go look for him, in whatever direction your magic tells us to. Do you really think we can find him?"

"Yes, yes, I do. We will find my brother and you two will reunite. I will dance at your wedding. Between the two of us, we will turn this into a Disney fairytale, not a Brothers' Grimm one." Niana laughed at the look on Teri's face. "Don't forget, I lived in the human world until I was eighteen. Even in the kemana, we couldn't avoid Disney movies. Now, we need to plan. Sean, are you coming with us?"

The Willen looked up from where he had been halfway dozing, "I don't know. What's in it for me? I brought Teri here to make sure that she had a bed and food because I felt responsible for her, but I have no reason to care about this guy. I know he's your brother, Niana, and her fiancé, but what do I get if I help?"

"I'll give you my iPad. When we were walking, you told me that human technology was worth a lot of money here, especially things like tablets and phones, so I'll give you mine. You can sell it." Teri pulled the tablet out of her pouch and held it out to Sean. "Please help us."

"Okay, I'll help, but not with anything dangerous."

The two women laughed, and Teri smiled at Sean. "We don't expect you to risk yourself but come along and help us search. Once we have a direction to look in."

"Okay, that I can do. Niana, I don't suppose we could maybe have dinner while we plan? That stew smells good, and we didn't get any 'cause Teri fainted."

"I didn't faint. I was overwhelmed and exhausted. But I agree that dinner would be wonderful. Niana, can we impose?"

"Definitely. I made enough for the three of us to eat. Come on, we'll have some stew, bread, and freshly brewed tea, and make some plans. Tomorrow, I'll do a tracking spell and hopefully, finally find out what happened to my brother. I do wonder why my parents didn't ask for help, though. Even if their magic wasn't strong enough on Earth, there are many Light Elves they could ask."

"Is there a kemana near Charlotte? They live in a suburb in Charlotte, North Carolina. There might not have been any way for them to contact someone to help them."

"You could be right. Oh, well, too late to wonder now. We will make it right. I expect an invitation to your wedding for finding him, though"

"Find him for me, help me rescue him from wherever he is, and you can be my maid of honor!"

"Deal!"

Talking animatedly amongst themselves, the three new friends went into the kitchen to eat and scheme, and a sense of purpose united them.

The next morning, Teri accompanied Niana as she travelled

through the village and the forest around it to gather the ingredients she would need for her spell. While the women searched for spell components, Sean took odds and ends that Teri had found in her belt pack and sold them on the black market to raise money for their journey. She would need new clothes, at least, to help her fit in. They would also all need travel packs and provisions to take with them, unless Marc turned out to be closer than they thought.

As the two women searched the market and forest for the necessary items, they talked, learned more about each other, and told stories about their lives. Teri was particularly enthralled by Niana's stories about the twins' childhood and the trouble they both got in to.

"So, let me get this straight, he actually made a cat fly?"

"Well, yes. But not intentionally. I adopted a kitten when we were six. It wandered in from the mundane world, and I fell in love with it. After much begging on my part, my parents let me keep her, but I couldn't let her leave the house without me. Einmarco—I mean Marc—and I wanted to go on an adventure, and I didn't want to leave Kit behind, so we took her with us. We went to the park and as cats do, she jumped from my shoulders and ran up a tree. The silly thing couldn't get down, so Marc decided to spell her down. Very seriously, he tried to levitate her from the tree branch so I could grab her. Instead, he gave her wings. She startled and flew away. Eventually, she came back, and my parents removed her wings, but after that, she always tried to get as high up as she could."

Teri laughed. "Poor kitten. I can imagine her expression. My Shadow would be horrified if that happened to him. He likes to keep all four paws on the ground, thank you very much. Hey, something I've meant to ask you...what's with the colored hair? Yours is purple, and you say Marc's is really dark-blue—why?"

"Because we're witches. We have colored hair but I'm not sure of the reason. Luckily, we can blend in with the human world since everyone seems to dye their hair." Niana stopped beside a patch of purple flowers the shade of her hair and clipped some to place in her basket. "Okay, this was the last ingredient. Now, I need to brew my potion and cast the spell. We'll have Marc back to you really soon. Let's see what Sean managed to buy." Still chatting, they headed back toward the house and Niana stopped occasionally to point things out to Teri that might interest her.

When they arrived, it was to find Sean sitting on the front porch with three laden traveler's packs. "It's about time you two got back. I've been here forever and I'm starving. What's for lunch? Oh, by the way, Teri, I bought you some new clothes. Not that you don't look fetching in Niana's, but she is three inches taller than you, and her skirts are too long. Plus, I thought you might prefer pants for travelling."

Teri thanked him and followed them as Niana led the way back into the house. When they reached the kitchen, she directed them in putting together a lunch of cheese, bread, sausage, and small olive-like vegetables. After they ate and helped to clear the dishes, Niana prepared the area for her brewing and spell work. "Teri, none of this will make much sense to you. Can you find something to do while I set up and prepare the potion?"

"Of course. I've been dying to read some of your books. They're in English, right?"

"Not most of them, but they do have translation spells on them, so you should be able to read them. The histories might interest you. I'll call you when I have some results. Enjoy. Feel free to take a nap. This will take me until moonrise, at least."

As Niana clipped and ground ingredients, Teri wandered into the living room to search through the books. Finding one on ancient Oriceran history, she settled in on the couch and was soon lost in the words. She didn't even notice when she fell asleep and the book dropped from her hand to the floor.

She woke to someone shaking her shoulder. "Teri, wake up. I found him! I found Marc. He's less than a day's journey from here. We need to make arrangements to leave first thing in the morning."

"Did you really find him, Niana? Is this nightmare really almost over?"

"Yes. Now all we have to do is go get him. On the plus side, the direction he is in is nowhere near Trevilsom, so he wasn't arrested as a portal jumper. And he's alive. The trace would have been different if all I found was a grave. We will find him—and find out what prevented him from going home. Come have some dinner. You need to try on the clothes Sean brought for you. Then we can pack and make our plans to set off tomorrow. I will need to make sure I bring some basic spell components and my wand with me."

"Okay. I'm not sure what I'll need, but I will trust you guys. Can you tell me more about Marc as a boy over dinner?"

"Gladly. Come on. You can help with dinner and we'll talk."

When they set out the next morning, the sun was still rising, and Teri couldn't restrain a series of yawns. She was excited about finally seeing Marc again but also terrified of what they might find. Even though Niana said the trace indicated that he was alive, it didn't confirm what condition he was in. What if he was injured? Worse, what if he wasn't and he had merely decided not to come back to her? She wanted closure, but she wasn't sure that she could handle him deliberately leaving her. Either way, though, she would finally know.

Following Niana and Sean through the woods, she took the time to look around her at the flowers and animals that they didn't have in her world. She finally had a chance to see the flowers in their natural habitat, and the way they swayed towards every sound enchanted her. Suddenly, a small, green, furry creature peeked out from behind a plant. When she stopped to look closer at it, Sean paused with her.

"I wouldn't if I were you. That's a troll. You do *not* want to adopt one. He'll eat you out of house and home. Plus, they link to your emotions, and if you are scared or in danger, he'll grow to be about eight feet tall—not exactly easy for you to hide in rural America."

"But it's so cute—"

"Yeah, but leave it be. So, any ideas about what you will say to Marc once we find him?"

"No. A lot of it depends on how we find him. What state he is in when we do."

"Well, you might want to think about it. At the pace we're walking, we'll be there by late afternoon. If you have words you want to say to him, you need to think of them now. We'll stop in an hour for lunch." Sean increased his pace and moved to walk beside Niana to give Teri some space to think and plan.

After another hour and a brief stop to eat bread and cheese from their packs, they resumed their journey and approached a small, fenced village in the woods a few hours before dusk. Niana cast a spell to conceal their approach and led the way around the outskirts of the settlement. As they neared the far side, an odd sight greeted them. Standing next to a wooden gate in the fence was a stone statue of a man poised to fight, his sword in hand. The witch ran up to it with a gasp.

"Teri, get over here. Please! It's Marc. This is why he didn't come back to you—he couldn't. He's been turned to stone. So close to my home... Why didn't anyone tell me? How could I have not known?" The purple-haired witch collapsed in tears, while Teri stood in shock before she succumbed to sobs beside her. Neither of the women noticed the Willen slip away to town until he returned almost thirty minutes later.

"I can tell you ladies why he's a statue. I went to the bar and asked around, and some gentlemen who were here eight years ago told me what happened. It was stupid and random, but it's also fixable. He was here looking for someone to open a portal for him, and when there was nobody here who would help, he left. He was in a real hurry to get back and said that he had already been gone for too long. When he walked out the gate, he stepped on a basilisk's tail. The creature reacted out of instinct and stoned him. Nobody knew who he was or who his family was, and they wouldn't pay the cost to heal him when there was no possibility, they thought, of reimbursement. So, they propped him up here to deter bandits."

"They left him to stand here? Let birds make a nest on his head and small animals shelter under him?" Niana fumed. "I can't believe they didn't heal him. It's such a simple fix, and he would have paid to be unpetrified. How can they be so mercenary?"

"Because that's what they are, love. Mercenaries and smugglers. Scoundrels, not so far from us and the way our acquaintances behave, to be honest."

"But—" As Niana started to argue, she was interrupted by Teri.

"You said it's an easy fix? Can you do it? Can you bring him back? Please, Niana, can this be reversed? I want him back. I can't believe he is standing here in front of me. This is not what I think of when someone says they were stoned."

"Yes. I can fix it. I'll need to brew a potion, but I actually have most of the ingredients with me, and the rest I can find in the woods. Don't worry, we will get him back—today. Let me get started."

She turned to her pack to gather the necessary potion ingredients but paused. "Thank you, Sean. I appreciate you getting that information for us. I was too distraught and honestly, would have hexed someone if they told me they were too mercenary to help my brother."

"It was nothing. Get started with that potion. Teri looks like she'll pass out again."

Niana bent her head to her task and enlisted the other woman's assistance to chop and stir. Just before dusk, she finished the brew. As the last rays of the sun touched the gate and the moon rose over the trees, she poured the potion over the statue's head and made sure to get it in all the folds of petrified cloth and wrinkles of stone flesh.

"All right, we are ready. Teri, stand back. This could get messy." Niana pulled her wand out and intoned the words of the spell. "Hunc petrification carnem et reducam. Ne ipsum Vivamus anathema respirare!" With a loud crack, the stone encasing Marc's body shattered, and he fell to his knees.

The two women rushed to his side and Teri reached him first. "Marc! Marc sweetheart, are you okay? Oh, my God, you're alive. I have missed you *so* much."

"Teri? What are you doing here? For that matter, where is here? What am I doing here? Is that my sister behind you? Is that a Willen? What the hell is going on?" Confused, Marc looked at the three people around him. Tripping over each other, they took turns to tell him what had happened to bring them all there. Finally, he stopped them. "You're telling me I've been gone for eight years? They declared me dead? You didn't marry someone else, did you?"

"Of course not. I can't believe your stories of magic were true. It is so strange to see that all the things you've told me about are real. Although it did take Sean a while to convince me I wasn't hallucinating. But enough about me. What happened? How did you wind up in Oriceran?"

"I was kidnapped. Well, sort of. An old friend tracked me down and asked for help. When I said no, he pushed me through the portal and told me he wouldn't allow me to return until I helped him. So, I did. But then the mage who was supposed to make the portal was arrested, and well, I went to find one on my own. I got stoned, literally. I am so sorry."

"It doesn't matter. We're together now. We can find someone

to portal us back to the park, and then we will figure out how to explain to the authorities where you've been for the last eight years. Let's get you back to Niana's. Do we want to camp, or should we risk the village?"

After unanimously voting to set up camp in the woods and away from the village, the four turned to go. As they did so, Teri asked, "What did your friend need help with?"

Marc grinned, "That's a long story for another time. Let's get to camp. I haven't eaten in eight years." Putting his arm around her, he guided her behind Niana and Sean into the sunset.

The End

AUTHOR NOTES

First, THANK YOU! Thank you for reading and hopefully, enjoying my story. I had a hard time finding an idea that I could run with this time, and then on a drive to Tennessee with my mom, it popped in my head, almost fully formed. But I still wasn't sure I should write it.

Eight years ago, my boyfriend dumped me, by text, on Valentine's Day. No warning, and with no arguments leading up to it. Just a text. **I'm moving out on Feb 28, where are you going to go?** I have never gotten any reason and no closure. I have missed this guy for eight years. I loved him—REALLY loved him. Not breathing would be easier than not loving him. I have attempted over these eight years to move on, with a modicum of success. But he has always been in the back of my head, and the question occurred to me—Teri's first question in this story. How long is long enough to grieve? How long before you stop feeling that hurt? Thus, a story was born.

Except, in this story, I decided that my character could get what I did not. Closure and a happy ending. That's why it finally saw the light of day.

Now that I have written this story, given Teri—and by extension, myself, closure—I have a folder full of other Oriceran stories to write for next time. So there better be more Oriceran Fans Write books. LOL.

I need to send a special thank you to Sarah Weir. When I decided to write this story in a week, she supported me. She was a cheerleader of unparalleled help. Between her and Tracy Byrnes, I was encouraged, pushed, and led to the finish line, barely under the wire. Thank you both. Maybe next time, I can put one of you in my story.

Last, I owe a huge thank you to Martha and Michael for letting us all play in your sandbox. This has been a thrilling ride.

Ad Aeternitatem!
Trae

BAYOU BOUNTY HUNTER

BY CHARLES TILLMAN

Matt Bordelon has spent all his adult life battling dark magic, first as a Silver Griffin and now as a government-sanctioned bounty hunter. One who's willing to do whatever it takes to bring in his bounty. He has it all figured out…until a dark witch stands his world on its head.

This is for all of you who helped me get here. Michael Anderle, Craig Martell, Justin Sloan, and Martha Carr, who inspired me to simply write something. Your examples of how it is done along with your words of encouragement helped me to put my self-doubt aside and put my writing out there for the world to see. To my wife and first beta reader for working through numerous rewrites and pointing out the good and the bad in each one. To two of my fellow authors who took the time out of writing their own stories to read mine and make suggestions to make it better. You know who you are, and your friendship and words of encouragement are what kept me going when I wanted to quit. Without all of you, I would have never had the courage to write or submit this. Thank you all for being my friends.

CHAPTER ONE

Matt Bordelon was one of the new breed of bounty hunters. With the revelation of Oriceran and that magic existed a few years back, the government had slowly begun to realize that traditional police tactics would not work for magical beings. That brought about changes to the justice system that allowed freelancers like Matt to make a nice living bringing in criminals who used magic. Taking down magical criminals was nothing new for him. As a former Silver Griffin, he had done it for years. The difference now was that he was paid well to do it.

Matt had started his career with the Silver Griffins after a magic incident shortly after graduating from Archbishop Rummel High School in Metairie, Louisiana. Raised by his paternal grandmother after his parents were both killed in an accident, he was the sole heir of an old and respected New Orleans family. His predecessors dated back to the early years when the settlement in French territory was small, and he grew up with all the privileges of old money. Private Catholic schools, chauffeured cars, a mansion in the garden district, society parties, and some of the best magic tutors money could buy.

"You come from old money and even older magic, boy.

Always remember, though, that with great power comes greater responsibility," his grandmother told him.

Matt had been warned all his life not to use magic where normals could see it. His grandmother and his tutors all drilled that into his head, but like any teen, he couldn't resist using it whenever he had the chance. Unfortunately, doing so on the corner of Bourbon and St. Peter in the French Quarter on a busy Saturday night was not the smartest move he could have made. He'd used a compulsion spell to make two obnoxious drunken tourists, who harassed a couple of young women, do a striptease in the middle of Bourbon Street. Although as funny as hell—and, truth be told, richly deserved—it was not his brightest moment.

How could he have known that a bachelorette party was in full swing at the Cat's Meow for one of the Midwest Silver Griffins? Or that Lacy Trader, the head of the Silver Griffins, would be belting out, "I Put A Spell On You," to the karaoke machine at the exact moment he zapped the two drunken idiots. Luckily for him, it was New Orleans, and that type of behavior was not really out of the norm—well, except that it was two cowboys from Austin doing the strip show. Hats, boots, big belt buckles, and all. To say that Trader was not amused was an understatement.

The fact that Lacy and his grandmother were friends was all that saved him from serious repercussions. Trader gave him two choices—join the Silver Griffins or go straight to Trevilsom Prison. Given those limited choices, the next-day hangover notwithstanding, Matt was paired with a crusty old wizard to learn things that made his previous magic training look like Sunday school at the local parish.

Regus Morningstar was an old-school wizard who had come to the Silver Griffins on a path similar to Matt's. He was the second son of one of the old dark families who was caught performing passion spells on girls when he was only nineteen. The Griffin who caught him in the act saw the possibility that he was more than simply a spoiled kid from a dark family. He thought the boy had potential, so he took him on as an apprentice in the early 1900s. Regus never told Matt which family he came from, only that he'd changed his name when he became a Griffin. When asked, he had replied that the person he was before was dead and buried in the past and best left there.

The old him might have been dead, but Regus had no problem using whatever spell was needed to get the job done. Matt's training was intense and had included a fair amount of magic that was most assuredly not on the Silver Griffins' approved list. Some of the spells his mentor taught him could have landed them both in serious trouble, but Regus always maintained that to fight monsters, you sometimes had to be scarier than them.

Matt had loved that old wizard like the father he never knew. When the dark families attacked the Griffins vault in Chicago, Regus had died defending the door. Matt saw it happen a split second before the ceiling came down but was unable to get a shot at the killer before he escaped. He was shocked when he later learned the identity of the killer. Winston Blackwell, the head of one of the more notorious dark families, was the older brother of Arthur Blackwell, who had gone by the name Regus Morningstar for the last hundred years.

His first instinct was to go in immediate pursuit, but he was forbidden to do so by the Silver Griffins because of the need to retrieve the stolen artifacts. He continued to work for the order until they disbanded shortly after the attack, but his heart was no longer in it. Matt returned home to New Orleans where he spent his time searching for the stolen artifacts and hunting Winston Blackwell. He never caught the killer, but he did see the aftermath of several crimes attributed to him.

When government agents approached him and suggested he become one of the first licensed bounty hunters, he signed up immediately and was soon a licensed level-six operative. The license was based on his previous experience as a Silver Griffin.

If the truth be told, he was a powerful wizard who could have been rated higher. His rationale was that if he stuck to bounties below his weight class, he could make a decent living and not be tempted to get in over his head. One of the first things Regus ever said to him had stayed with him throughout his career with the Griffins and as a bounty hunter.

"Matt, to survive this, you need to remember one thing. There are old wizards, and there are bold wizards, but there are very few old bold wizards."

CHAPTER TWO

Matt smiled as he stepped out into the crisp evening air. He had just dropped off a level-four bounty at the Knox County jail in Knoxville, Tennessee, and his bank account was already fatter. *Damn, it sure is nice to do business with folks who have their shit together where bounties are concerned. It took them less than twenty minutes from the time I dropped his ass off at the jail to pay me.*

This bounty, unbeknownst to the police, had been bilking retirees of their life savings with the use of an Oriceran artifact. He'd even dared to use it on the Knoxville detectives when they came to see him. That stunt had jumped him up to a level-four and earned him a very special place in the hearts of the local cops.

Matt being there by invitation probably helped too. It seemed the Chief of Detectives of Knoxville and the head of the New Orleans Magical Action Unit were both Fraternal Order of Police members who had known each other for years. Of course, Lt. Julien LeDoux had nothing but good things to say about Matt Bordelon—who had also happened to call him Uncle Julien for most of his life. Of course, it helped that he was a talented New

Orleans bounty hunter with a reputation for bringing in some of the worst criminals around.

The takedown of this particular bounty turned out to be relatively easy. Once Matt talked to a few of his victims, he determined that he used magic to convince people to do whatever he told them. This could be to invest in a scam hedge fund or, in the case of the cops, that he wasn't there when they confronted him. If it hadn't been for the drone they had tracked him with, they would never have caught on that something was amiss. The two investigators, following close on his heels, went into his office and exited minutes later. When they claimed the suspect wasn't there, authorities knew this was no ordinary crook. That little stunt was the real reason he had a level-four, breathing optional bounty. It seems that Knoxville cops took having magic used on them very seriously.

Matt laughed as he thought back to the shocked look on the bounty's face when he confronted him. He held his fist out, a smirk on his face, and his lips moved ninety to nothing as he tried to spell Matt. The bounty hunter merely walked up, punched him between the eyes, and knocked him out cold. When he came to, he was trussed up like a Christmas turkey, minus the silver artifact shaped like an old cheerleader megaphone he used to influence his victims. The expression on his face when Matt went all *Jason and The Argonauts* and plucked the wax earplugs out of his ears was priceless. Now, Matt was a few thousand richer and had an artifact in his pocket that could prove useful on future jobs.

It was a pretty night in Knoxville, so Matt decided to walk to the Starbucks over on the University of Tennessee campus to catch the train back to New Orleans. He enjoyed the sights, smells, and cooler weather of the city but was immediately distracted when a black orb shot through with red streaks rocketed into the night from the stadium parking lot. Cautiously, he moved closer. Two cloaked figures in the shadow of the stadium hurled powerful dark spells at each other. It was apparent that they attempted to do some lethal damage from the type of magic they slung. Ever the opportunist, Matt continued his furtive approach, hoping there was a bounty on one or both. His best plan would be to let them fight it out, ambush the victor, and bag them both.

He was close enough to hear them from where he crouched behind the fender of a truck. From their voices, he could tell the combatants were a man and a woman. He listened in to what they were saying using an artifact that filtered out ambient noise and brought the speech in as clearly as if he stood beside them.

"I am not some broodmare Mother can marry off to the highest bidder. Remy Blackmore is a womanizing, abusive bastard, and I will never marry him, no matter what you or Mommy Dearest want!" she screamed as she launched a thick stream of red flame toward the man.

He batted it aside with a careless shrug. "You don't have a choice, Natalia. Your opinion of Remy and your objections are duly noted, but you will not bring shame to our family. Mother worked hard to arrange this pairing, and it will increase our family standing with the other dark families. You either come back to Lexington willingly, or I'll blast you until you are too weak to resist. You know you can't beat me. You never have and never will."

"Dammit, Chauncey! Why do you always have to be such a prick? Mommy's favorite, always doing her bidding. Grow a pair and tell her you couldn't find me."

"Okay, that's enough of this stupidity. If you were half as loyal to our family as I am, you would not have run, and we wouldn't be here. If you don't come back on your own, I will do whatever is necessary before I let you shame us in the eyes of the others." As he spoke, a large globe of black formed on the tip of his wand and he raised it menacingly above his head. "Last chance, sister. What will it be? Marriage or death?"

She responded with a cluster of small black orbs that split apart and careened toward the wizard as she grunted, "Marrying that bastard will be the death of me, and you damn well know it." As the orbs approached, he threw his hand out. They stopped and reversed course toward the witch. She tried desperately to block them, but one struck her hand and dislodged her wand, and another impacted her shoulder and thrust her into a wall.

"Well, Natalia, since you are determined not to honor your obligations to the family—something Mother thought was possible—it's up to our dear sister Angelica to step up and do it for you. She always was the more loyal daughter. The fact that she has been screwing Remy for the past two years makes me sure he would rather have her instead of your ungrateful ass anyway." He laughed as he prepared to release the massive ball of dark magic toward her. It was a death spell, and without her wand, she was utterly helpless to stop it.

She lay there, stunned, and as she struggled to stand, her hood fell away to provide Matt his first look at her. He was struck by how hopeless she looked but that was soon overshadowed by the fact that she was the most beautiful woman he had ever seen. Even with dirt smudges on her face and wearing scorched and tattered clothes, she was gorgeous with her dark hair with a pair of the deepest-green eyes he had ever seen. High cheeks, full lips, and porcelain skin reminded him of some of the drawings which depicted how humans had imagined elven beauties looked before the truth came out about elves and other beings from Oriceran. Matt's wand was in his hand as if it had a mind of its own and a spell he had never dared use came to his lips. In that moment, he had no thought of consequence, only an overwhelming instinctual need to protect this woman.

The wizard stood poised to release his spell at the helpless woman, but a thin black line exploded from the tip of Matt's wand. It was a spell designed to penetrate any shield—an assassin's spell—and drew on some of the blackest magic Regus had ever taught him. The old man had told him there was no defense against it and cautioned him to only use it in the direst of emergencies. The narrow beam caught the wizard in the back of the head at the moment that he flung the orb. It didn't completely stop the spell from reaching the prone woman, but it did dissipate it enough that she only suffered a glancing blow. Her body slid across the pavement and slammed into the unyielding wall behind her with a sickening thud.

Matt ran to her and rolled her over. Blood trickled from her mouth and nose, but he could see she was still breathing. He checked her pulse anxiously and found that it was beating steadily, and he breathed a sigh of relief, knowing that she was still alive and hopefully not hurt too badly. He turned to the prostrate wizard, but dull, lifeless eyes stared at him, a pencil-thin blackened hole directly between them where his spell had exited.

The bounty hunter formed a portal that opened over a moonlit body of water surrounded by ancient cypress trees draped in Spanish moss. With a grunt, he heaved the body unceremoniously through the gateway and before the ripples from the splash had even settled, multiple dark shapes glided through the water toward it.

I hope those 'gators don't get sick when they eat his sorry ass.

He closed the portal with a snap of sparks and immediately went down on his knees and gasped for air. His vision went dark as his body reeled from bone-numbing exhaustion.

Damn, now I see what Regus meant when he told me not to use that spell unless I was sure there were no other threats around. Okay, Bordelon, you got this. Get your ass up and do what you got to do. You ain't gonna let one dark spell knock you on your ass like some weak little bitch. Move your ass!

Matt continued the internal monologue as he struggled to his feet. He lurched to the prone figure on shaky knees, picking up her wand and stuffing it in his pocket on the way. He fell to his knees again, breathing hard, and shook his head to try to dispel the dizziness. After a deep breath, he was barely able to open another portal, this one providing entry into a softly-lit room lined with shelves of books. He wanted to carry the girl but was unable to stand, let alone lift her. Instead, he grabbed her collar and dragged her behind him as he crawled through the portal into the study of his house in New Orleans.

CHAPTER THREE

Natalia woke with a start and pushed herself up as a wave of nausea swamped her. She screwed her eyes shut and took several deep breaths as she fought through it. Slowly, she opened her eyes to find that she was on an oversized plush couch in a room she didn't recognize. The events of the night before rushed back, and her stomach tried to rebel again.

Chauncey tried to kill me! Where am I and how am I still alive? More importantly, how do I get out of here?

She stood shakily and started to move away from the couch but immediately met with resistance—like she tried to walk through water up to her neck. As she fought against it, the strength increased until she was knocked back onto the couch by a sharp electric jolt. She lay there, her body tingling from the shock, and noticed a thin white chalk line drawn on the floor in front of her. She traced it with her eyes and dread coiled within as she realized she was in a containment spell, and a powerful one at that.

Matt woke to the sound of a bell tolling in his head. He tried to tune it out and doze off, but it persisted. He jerked awake as he realized it was the alarm on the ward he had put around the witch. She was up and had tried to leave the circle. He blinked several times to clear his eyes and was finally able to see his watch, although blearily, and released a tortured groan as he saw that he had managed a whole two hours of sleep. Mumbling under his breath about the many faults of early risers, he stumbled to the kitchen to put on some much-needed coffee. Dealing with a potentially pissed-off and dangerous dark witch most definitely required coffee. As the scent of the strong brew with a hint of chicory filled the air, he mused for probably the thousandth time that if coffee tasted like it smelled, it would cost a thousand dollars a cup.

While it brewed, he stepped into the bathroom for a cold shower to help clear his head. His teeth chattered from the cold and he toweled off quickly, dressed, and was back in the kitchen as the brew completed. He poured a cup and breathed in the aroma of good New Orleans coffee, made with loving care by a true Cajun roastmaster. After a satisfying sip, he poured a second cup and snatched a couple of packs of sugar and artificial creamer that he had pocketed from a Starbucks on the off chance that he might someday have a guest who was barbarian enough to ruin good coffee.

She sat with her back to him when he stepped into the room. The containment circle he used kept the person inside entirely isolated with no sound in or out. It was a handy feature when you needed to discuss a prisoner without them listening in. It also prevented attracting unwanted attention when holding them in a less-than-private location. Matt really could do without police snooping around because some busybody neighbor thought they heard screaming coming from his house…again.

He stepped slowly around to where he could see her profile and was again struck by how beautiful she was. Her once-white shirt that showed barely a hint of pale cleavage was scorched and blood-stained, and her long, dark hair was a tangled mess framing her blood-spattered face, but she was still gorgeous. As he moved into view, she recoiled from him. Her eyes were wide, and fear was evident on her face. Matt felt an uncontrollable desire to protect this woman. He wanted to wrap her in cotton and keep her from ever being hurt again.

Cool yourself down now, Bordelon. You don't know anything about this girl except that she was in a magic firefight and threw some potent dark spells. Remember, pretty things in nature are often the most deadly.

Natalia stared intently at the man who was her apparent jailor. *Who is this guy? I don't know him, but he does look scrumptious —dark hair, not too short but the perfect length to run your fingers through, and those eyes—I don't think I have ever seen eyes that blue. Oh, my God. What the ever-loving fuck are you thinking, Nat? You're his prisoner and for all you know, he's working for your douche of a brother.*

Matt pulled a chair in front of the couch and moved a small table between them. She seemed to calm a little at this and looked more confused than scared. Her lips moved as she talked but he was unable to hear her through the ward. A quick wave of his wand lifted the noise-canceling part of the spell.

"—are you? Why am I here? What are you planning to do to me? I can pay you..." She slowly ran out of steam and watched expectantly as Matt took a slow sip from his mug, his eyes closed in absolute bliss as the rich dark roast tantalized his taste buds. He sighed contently and opened his eyes.

"Good mornin', cher. I hope you slept well. I'm sure you have all kinds of questions, but before we get to that, please tell me one thing." He smiled as he watched her over the steaming cup.

"Who... Why...what is it you want?" she finally managed to say.

"Black, or cream and sugar?" He gestured at the second steaming cup on the table.

"Huh?"

"Coffee, cher. Do you use cream, sugar, or do you take it black?"

Understanding dawned as she mumbled, "Black. Please."

"Okay. Now, I'm gonna' open the circle but know this. If you try anything dumb, I will defend myself." She looked surprised but quickly nodded her agreement. *Provided he doesn't give me a reason.*

With a wave of his wand, the spell dissipated with a pop, and he gestured toward the cup. Natalia picked it up and held it under her nose to inhale the aroma. Her eyes closed slowly as she savored the tantalizing smell.

She brought the cup hesitantly to her lips and took a tentative sip. Her eyes widened as the flavors of rich dark-roasted coffee and a hint of something she didn't recognize exploded across her taste buds.

"Oh, Lord, that is good. I have never tasted anything like it before. What is that flavor?" She held the cup to her nose and breathed in the aroma before she took another slow sip and savored the exquisite brew.

"That's a little taste of New Orleans, cher. It's a local flavor unique to the area called chicory. We Cajuns been adding that to coffee here since the French settled." He smiled. "Mardi Gras, ettoufee, gumbo, beignets, barbequed shrimp, and coffee with chicory. The things that make New Orleans, New Orleans."

Natalia giggled at the passion he had for his city, but she caught herself focusing on how his eyes sparkled as he told her about things she had heard of but that he loved. Again, she cautioned her inner self that she did not know who this person was or what his intentions were. A good cup of coffee, gorgeous blue eyes, and a sexy-ass accent did not mean he was a good man.

"So, do you want to tell me why that wizard did his dead-level damnedest to kill you last night, cher?"

She startled at the quick change of subject and the fire in his eyes as he said it. His demeanor went from playful and friendly to cold and dangerous in an instant.

A haunted look settled in her eyes and she hesitated as she took a steadying breath before answering. "It was a family dispute. My mother sent him to bring me home, and when I refused, he tried to kill me."

"That's harsh, cher. Why would he try to kill you for not comin' home?"

Natalia looked into his eyes again and saw a warmth that made her feel she could trust him. She didn't know why—trust wasn't normal for any member of the dark families, and particularly not hers—but she felt that even though he might not be a good man, he didn't mean to hurt her.

"First off, I'm Natalia Greymont of the Lexington, Kentucky, Greymonts. The wizard who tried to kill me is my older brother, Chauncey. When my father died, my mother took over as head of the family and entered into a pact with Winston Blackwell that I would marry his oldest son. Remy Blackwell is a no good, womanizing, evil bastard. I ran away and hid in Knoxville until I could decide what to do. I didn't hide well enough, and Chauncey caught up with me last night. He said if I didn't perform my family duty, he would kill me and that my slut of a sister Angelica would happily marry him to seal the pact between our families.

"I remember him disarming me, and the last thing I saw was the spell coming toward me, then I woke up here." She whispered softly, "So now that you know who I am, will you be so kind as to tell me who the hell you are and why I'm here?"

Matt's heart ached for the woman and the pain she was going through as he considered how much to tell her. Knowing that Winston Blackwell was involved made him even more cautious.

"Okay, cher. My name is Matt—Matthew Bordelon—and I'm a licensed bounty hunter. I was up in Knoxville on a bounty and was makin' my way to the train station when I saw you two goin' at each other in the stadium. I knew you were both black magic users by the spells you were slingin', so I snuck up on the fight in hopes of picking up an easy bounty or two. I brought you here after, made sure you weren't hurt too bad, and passed out. That was about two hours ago."

"Well, Mr. Bordelon, to my knowledge, there are no bounties on me. I suppose that means I'm free to go?"

"Cher, I'm not plannin' to hold you against your will, but if your brother found you, I'm thinkin' you need to figure out a better way to hide so you don't be found again. It looks like your family likes to play rough." Matt's accent grew stronger as he spoke.

"I don't want to bring my problems to you. Thank you for helping me, but I really shouldn't stay here. You don't want my brother coming here for me. He is one of the most powerful wizards of this generation and has no qualms about hurting anyone who gets in his way."

"Oh, cher, you don' need t' worry none 'bout me. I promise you that the chances of anybody findin' you here are slim to none. I also can assure you that they would not live long enough t' regret it if they attacked here." The last emerged with cold certainty.

"Be that as it may, I don't want to be a problem for you after you saved my life. By the way, how did you get me away from Chauncey? I've seen him use that spell before and it is lethal one hundred percent of the time."

"I hit him from behind while he was focused on killing you. He never saw me, so I was able to knock his aim off enough that he didn't manage a solid hit."

"He will hunt you for that. Chauncey does not take being beaten by anyone, and he will be after you with murder on his mind." Her voice rose and grew more panicked as she spoke.

"Cher, you really shouldn't worry your pretty self none bout' that. Chauncey won't be botherin' you or me no more, I guarantee."

"You don't know what you're dealing with here—and who the hell is Cher? I told you my name is Natalia," she snapped.

Matt felt his cheeks flush as he realized he had called her cher, a Cajun term of endearment, through the conversation.

"I'm sorry, Natalia, cher is a local thing we use when talking here. It don't mean nothing," he lied.

"Whatever. Look, Matt, you seem like a nice guy, but you do not know my brother. He will not rest until finds and kills you—and me for that matter."

He was torn between telling her the truth about her brother and keeping it to himself. She seemed to hate him, but Matt knew that family often trumped hate when someone else was involved in the fight. He was still running an internal debate when his phone played the theme song from the old TV show *Cops*. He snatched the device up, knowing that it was the New Orleans Police.

"Bordelon. What you got for me?"

"And good mornin' to you too, Matthew. I'm doin' just fine, thank you very much. Have you been by to see your granmama lately? I saw her at Mass on Saturday, and she was tellin' me how her ingrate of a grandson was too busy to come see a poor old woman," the heavily accented voice on the other end chided with a laugh.

"Mornin', Uncle Julien. I'm sorry, I'm a little distracted this mornin'. I promise I'll go see grandmama soon as I can. So, what can I do for the fine men in blue of New Orleans today?"

"We got a wizard fella down at Harrah's who was cheatin' at the roulette wheel. When security caught on and went after him, he tried to portal out. Harrah's put that spell what blocks portals since they got robbed last year, so he started slingin' fire and took off runnin'. He's been drinkin' all night and is drunker than a possum in the mash barrel. He holed hisself up in a bathroom off the casino floor and now, the bastard throws fire at anybody who gets close. Harrah's put the funds up for a level-four to get him out of there. There's an extra hundred grand bonus if it can be done without burnin' the place to the ground. Figured you would want this one since it's only three miles from your house," Lt. Julien LeDoux told him.

"Okay, Unc, I'll head on down in a few. I need to tie somethin' up here before I go."

As he disconnected the call, he looked up and saw Natalia glaring at him with a furious scowl on her face.

"I don't give a damn who you think you are or that you did save my life. There is no way in hell you are tying me up, Mr. Bordelon," she spat.

Matt stepped back, confusion written on his face as he looked at the fiery woman before him. He thought back on the conversation and laughed. "No, no, cher, I didn't mean I was gonna tie you up. It's another local thing. What we need to do is figure out where we stand. I told you, I won't hurt you or keep you here if you want to go, but I do want you to stay here a spell. Only until we decide what we got to do to keep people from finding you again."

"I don't know." She sighed. "If my brother catches me here, he'll kill us both, and I don't want to see you hurt because of me."

"I told you that you don't have to worry about that here. This house is layered with some of the best protection around. Hell, any magical being who tries to step onto the grounds uninvited will get their ass knocked into the middle of next week. Anyone who messes with me here dies. I wasn't foolin' none about that, cher."

Natalia sucked in her lower lip as she thought, and Matt decided that was the cutest thing he had ever seen.

He realized that he had it bad for this girl he knew next to nothing about, but for some reason, he didn't care.

"So you what? Want me to stay here while you run off to do your bounty thing? What, like a good little wife?" she fumed.

"Well, cher, I don't think you would ever be a 'good' little wife in the traditional sense." He chuckled. "But I would appreciate it if you at least waited till I got back and we discussed some options to keep your pretty self away from your family and breathin'. If that's okay with you."

Wow, he certainly sounds like he wants me to stay. I don't know if he can stand up to my family, but he sure seems to think he can. If confidence was power, this guy would be unstoppable, and that sexy accent that leaks out when he gets excited...oh, my God.

"If you're sure me being here is safe, I guess it wouldn't hurt to stay for a little while." Natalia lowered her head, conflicted by the strong attraction she felt for this man she hardly knew.

Matt sighed with relief. "Okay, I don't expect this to take long. It's only a drunk who got caught cheating at Harrah's. He probably got scared when security come up on him and now, he's looking for a way out. Stay inside, and you can have the run of the house. Any locked doors are warded, just so you know. The bath is at the end of the hall if you want to clean up. There are clean towels and I put some clothes out for you. We can get you something nicer when I get back. You go ahead and make yourself at home. I'll be back before you know it." The words emerged in a rush as he hurried toward the door and snatched a worn leather jacket from a chair as he went past.

"Oh, and don't try to go outside just yet, cher. The wards I told you about on the house won't be none too friendly to you if you do."

"Wait a minute. You said you wouldn't keep me here if I wanted to leave," she huffed.

"I won't be long, promise. We'll get this all worked out and reset them wards when I get back," he yelled as he ran out and slammed the door behind him.

She still stood speechless when she heard a loud engine fire up, and when she looked out the window, he barreled down the drive in tight jeans and a sexy black leather jacket, his hair blowing in the wind, astride a big black motorcycle.

CHAPTER FOUR

"Where ya at, Matt?"

"Kick his ass, Matthew."

"Yo, Matt, sup?"

The friendly greetings from the cops as Matt dismounted his bike was another New Orleans oddity. Police in other places viewed magic-using bounty hunters as a necessary evil, something needed but not to be fully trusted. In New Orleans, the revelation that magic was a real thing barely caused a ripple. Magic, in the form of voodoo and it's darker New Orleans bastard child Hoodoo, had been part of daily life for hundreds of years. Many of the police officers carried charms or even had Gris Gris bags in pockets or on strings around their necks.

When the truth came out about Matt, few batted an eyelid. He was Lt. LeDoux's nephew, the little kid who used to come by the station with fresh baked cakes and cookies from his grandmother. Many of the current cops were also legacies, meaning that their fathers, grandfathers, or both had worked at NOPD and had grown up fishing, hunting, and going to department family functions with Matt all his life. He was merely one of the family as far as they were concerned.

He approached a grey-haired officer and gave him a quick hug as he asked, "What we got here, Uncle Julien?"

"Dis fucker done got into the bathroom and chunks fire at anybody who pokes their head in is what we got, Matthew."

"Okay, Unc, I got this. Tell them I'm coming in and to get their heads down if they want to keep 'em."

"You be careful in there, boy, and dis bounty gets paid if he be breathin' or not when you done. Don't you be takin no chances and breakin' your granmamas heart. You hear me, boy?"

"Okay. What's this asshole's name anyway?"

"Billy Dedeaux from down in LaPlace. That's what the casino folks tol' us anyhow."

Matt stepped through the sliding doors onto the casino floor and whistled softly as he saw the damage inside. *Yeah, I bet they don't care if he's alive when this is over. Them slots aren't cheap, and it looks like he took out about twenty of those Double Diamonds, and the sprinklers aren't doing the rest of 'em much good either.*

He slogged through the artificial storm caused by the fire sprinklers and as he approached the bathroom door, he raised a shield. As he watched the water slough off the barrier, he kicked himself for not thinking to do that sooner.

"Hey, Billy, where ya' at?" he yelled from behind a row of fire- and water-damaged slot machines.

The answer was a small ball of fire that burst through the crack and into the machine he hid behind. A panicked voice yelled, "I done told you cops to stay the fuck away. I'm gonna' walk out of here and if you know what's good for you, nobody better get in my way."

"Yo, Billy, I don't be no cop," Matt yelled back.

"Well, then, who the hell you be?"

"It's Matt. Why don't you come on out of there and let me buy you a drink? We can talk this out over a shot or three."

"Matt? Matt Bordelon? Aw *hell* naw. I know who you are and there ain't no way in hell I'm comin' out of here so you can take me in." A half a dozen softball-sized fireballs homed in on Matt like guided missiles as Billy yelled his reply.

The bounty hunter didn't flinch as his shield repelled them in different directions. The additional damage to the gaming machines was merely collateral damage and he would be paid either way.

"Now, Billy, there don't need to be none of that. Let's work this out before you go getting yourself killed or something."

"I ain't comin' out of here. Now you go on and git, you hear?"

Matt rolled his eyes as he retrieved a small silver object from his pocket and gripped it tightly. *Well, I guess I'll see how this thing works.* He called, "Billy Dedeaux, you bring your ass out of there and stop this shit, *now!*"

Nothing happened, and he wondered if he had to be in sight of the person for it to work. He'd all but decided that he would have to go in after the drunken wizard when shuffling noises issued from behind the door. He raised his wand and summoned a medicine-ball-sized orb of white flame in preparation but let it dissipate with a laugh when he saw a skinny, middle-aged man wearing a faded old LSU cap and a Drew Brees Jersey step out of the door with a vacant look in his eyes.

Matt beckoned him over and plucked a worn cypress wand from his limp fingers. Calmly, he marched him out the door and into waiting arms of the NOPD Magical Action Squad.

As the bounty hunter walked toward his bike, he was inundated with pats on the back and congratulations from the officers gathered around. He called to the ones he knew, most of them by first name, as he made his way to his ride.

"Look, fellas, I would love to stay and chat, but I got something going right now and need to get back to it," he called as he climbed on the bike. "Unc, I will come by in a while and finish the paperwork on this one. But don't you let them casino people try to take damages out of my bounty when they see what he done to the place." He laughed.

"I got your back, boy. Who she be that got you runnin' off before you get paid?" the old man teased.

"It's work stuff, Unc. Don't you go telling Granmama no lies now. You know she's been on me to find a nice girl and settle down," Matt called as the engine roared to life.

"Hell, boy, she don't care if it be a nice girl or not by now. Any girl would do her," he shouted as Matt turned onto Poydras St. and sped toward home.

CHAPTER FIVE

"Oh, my!" Natalia exclaimed as she stepped into the bathroom. There was a garden tub big enough for three people with a gazillion jets in the sides and bottom. *That looks like heaven on earth.* She ran her hand along the rim. A basket of assorted soaps and bottles sat on the ledge, and when she looked closer, they were all from different chain hotels. She laughed at the selection that screamed bachelor and dispelled her initial impression that he had a wife.

As the steaming hot water filled the tub, she peeled off her scorched and tattered clothes. She took a hard look at herself in the mirror and saw that her body showed a roadmap of the fight she'd had with Chauncey. A scrape on her left shoulder had scabbed over. Bruises traced down her right side where she had struck the support. There were burns on both arms, her lips were split and swollen, and a puffy black eye completed the sorry spectacle.

Damn, I look disgusting, how could he even look at me without turning away? I am so going to kill my dickhead brother for this. What a way to make an impression on that oh so sexy man. Slow your roll, girl! *You just met this guy, and you know* nothing *about him. Stop acting like a lovesick schoolgirl and get your shit together,* she admonished herself again.

The warm water and soothing motion of the jets in the tub felt heavenly on her bruised and battered body. She slid into the water until only her face was above it and her long hair formed a dark halo as it floated around her head. Her eyes closed, and she had to hook her arm over the edge to keep from going under as she let the pulsing water leech the ache from her body.

She never heard the front door open.

CHAPTER SIX

When Matt walked in, he found the room where he had left Natalia empty. He made his way quietly through the house until he reached the partially closed bathroom door, peered through the gap, and caught a flash of pale skin. An arm hung limply over the edge of the tub with no sign of the girl attached. He burst through the door, fearing the worst, and was met with an indignant squawk from the furious naked woman who surged up from the bottom of the tub. Water sprayed across the room and splashed his boots.

"*What the fuck?*" she yelled with fire in her eyes.

"I-I-I'm sorry, cher," he stuttered, his eyes wide, unable to tear them away from the sight before him. "I thought something was wrong. I came in and didn't see you—when I looked in the door all I could see was your arm. I thought you had drowned or somethin'."

"*Get. Out. Now! You damned pervert!*" she screamed when she saw his gaze fixed on the bare breast she tried to cover without success.

Matt turned away, his face red with embarrassment, and fled into the kitchen to escape her wrath. He slumped into a chair with his head held between his hands, distraught by the encounter with Natalia.

Damn, boy, you done went and did it now. She thinks you're a sex fiend, tryin' to sneak a peek at her in the bath. But hot damn, what a peek it was. That's one fine woman!

"Did you get your eyeful, *Mister* Bordelon?" Natalia asked as she stormed into the kitchen.

"I'm so, so sorry, cher. I promise I wasn't tryin' to see you in the bath. I truly did think somethin' was wrong and I freaked," he stuttered, incapable of coherent speech.

When he raised his eyes, he beheld a vision of beauty starring daggers at him. Her wet hair soaked the light gray t-shirt she wore, and it outlined both breasts perfectly. His breath caught in his throat and it was all he could do to bring his gaze up to her eyes. The memory of the temptation he had seen earlier had permanently seared into his brain. He bit his tongue, afraid to speak lest anything he said would drive her away before he ever had the chance to prove himself to her.

"Look, cher, you don't know me, and I don't know you, but I know I would like the chance to get to know you better."

She continued to glare at him as what he had said slowly filtered through her anger.

What does he mean? He can't be he seriously saying what I think he said.

The fire faded from her eyes. Her face flashed through a series of emotions that ended with confusion.

She hesitated slightly before whispering, "Matt, it's...it's too dangerous. My brother—"

"No, cher, you don't have nothin' to fear from your brother ever again."

"You don't understand. He will never stop hunting me. Being around me will get you killed, and I couldn't live with myself if that happened," she murmured and blushed a deep red as she realized that she had said that out loud.

Matt's heart fluttered at this and he decided he had to tell her the truth about the night before. "Cher, I wasn't completely straight with you about everything that happened last night."

She took a hesitant step back, not sure what he meant.

He hurried on before he changed his mind. "I know for a fact that you don't have to be scared of Chauncey ever again. I did a little more than spoil his aim. I killed him with the deadliest magic I know and dumped his body through a portal deep into Honey Island Swamp. The only way he can ever threaten you again is if he can piece himself back together out of about a hundred pounds of gator shit."

She stood there speechless and various emotions coursed through her as she digested his words. "Is he truly gone? Are you sure he won't be back? How can you be sure?" She looked at him and a glimmer of hope shone through.

Matt said nothing as he drew his wand and opened a small portal in the air. It showed a black body of water surrounded by ancient moss-covered trees. An eighteen-foot-long alligator floated past in the dark water. "Because, cher, the 'gators in Honey Island Swamp never let go of a free meal," he murmured as he allowed the portal to slowly fade closed.

The End

AUTHOR NOTES

Thank You so much for reading this story and for continuing to read these author notes. Sarah Weir said I had to write some author notes at the end of the submission, and this is a first for me—so what to say? (Admin Edit: Yup, totally twisted your arm about it) -Sarah

Well, I am currently sitting in Las Vegas waiting impatiently for the 2018 20booksto50k-Vegas conference to start. If someone had told me I would write a story and actually put it out there for the world to see a year ago, I would have told them they were crazy. I have always been an avid reader but what could ever make me think I could write anything that someone else would want to read? I never felt that I had the experience, education, knowledge, or insert your favorite self-doubt word or phrase here (you get the picture), to try anything like this.

This all started when I came across a book a little over a year ago by someone called an indie writer. What the hell is an indie writer? It was some fellow by the name of Michael Anderle. It was a surprisingly good book. There were vampires, werewolves, space aliens, and all kinds of stuff that I liked to read about—*all in the same book!* I was hooked. I binge-read every one of his books and couldn't get enough.

I even read his author notes, something I seldom if ever did in the past, and learned that he was about my age and was not a journalism major or the like. Heck, he was a computer guy, and he had written a series of books that were some of the best I had ever seen. I responded to his invitation to follow him on Facebook and one day, when I had finished a book, I sent him a message to tell him how much I liked it and he messaged me back immediately. That blew my mind. The author wrote back to me in real time. Long story short, we continued to message back and forth from time to time and then I saw something about a group called 20booksto50k in a post. Being curious, I joined the group and found it was a whole lot of people who love to read and tell stories. They were some of the nicest and most interesting people I had ever met, and I knew I wanted to be a part of that tribe.

So that is how this author was born. I hope you enjoyed this short story and I look forward to writing more. If there was anything you particularly liked or even hated, please leave it in a review. Reviews are the fuel that runs this beast, and your comments, criticisms, and suggestions are what make all this possible.

Again, thank you for reading and a huge thank you to Michael Anderle and Martha Carr for creating this world and letting me play in it.

You can find me at

http://www.cftillman.com or on

Facebook at https://www.facebook.com/CFTillman

TROLLMANITY

BY LOGAN CAIRD

A hungry troll is a force to be reckoned with. All the more so when that Troll is caring for a litter of puppies and their mom. When put in that situation, there's really only one option…adventure!

DEDICATION

I want to dedicate this to everyone who has ever inspired me. That list is huge, but it starts with my parents and includes about thirty authors, many of whom are participating in and/or helping with this very Fan's Write. I want to also specifically thank Michael Anderle and Martha Carr for letting us play in their wonderful sandbox.

CHAPTER ONE

The troll was mostly called "get out of here," "what the hell are you?" or some variation of an incoherent scream, but he thought of himself as Beaty. He ran his hands through the matted hair of the momma dog he sat beside. He called her Sandy because no-one else gave her a name. The half-dozen puppies suckled voraciously. They were plump and energetic, but their mother looked gaunt. Beaty could see her ribs outlined against her fur and he didn't think that was a good thing.

Sandy jerked as one of her offspring bit down hard, then laid her head down once more. She didn't have the energy to really do much more than nudge the puppies out of the way.

He pushed the transgressor aside to give the others more room. At this point, the puppies were larger than him and would need to switch to solid food soon. This wasn't the first time he had helped the momma dog with a litter, although he was worried because he'd never seen her this weak and debilitated before.

It had been at least a few days since she'd moved from her position. She'd given up on trying to keep track of the young ones herself and left it to Beaty, which was why they were all gathered in this corner of the building. So far, they hadn't managed to jump over the wall of rubble he'd set up around their sleeping area. He had to repair it every few hours to make sure it kept them in, but even if he left, they should still be stuck there with their momma for long enough for him to get back.

One of the puppies hopped onto Sandy and vaulted from there at the wall of rubble. It scrambled halfway up and tumbled down, rolled over the rest of the dogs, and landed with its big floppy head resting against Beaty's legs. He burst out laughing and ruffled its ears. Then and there, he decided to call *that* puppy Bounder.

He pushed to his feet and crawled past the dogs, over the crumbling section of wall, and up the inside of the abandoned building they squatted in. With practiced ease, he swung out a broken window and onto a rusted rooftop.

At a glance, he could see that the trash bin in the alley down below had been emptied too recently to have anything worthwhile in it. Beaty slid down a pipe, trotted to the end of the alley, and became a somewhat emaciated golden retriever in the process. He looked almost exactly like a male version of the mother dog he'd left. His hair was a little less matted, his fur cleaner, and his ribs were more padded but still visible.

A bike—much quieter than he would have expected—hurtled past the alley at the same moment as he stuck his head out.

The rider shouted something unintelligible and kicked Beaty, and the impact skidded him back to bounce against the garbage bin. He scrambled up and barked after him, but the rider was a fair distance away and didn't slow. The troll-retriever pursued for almost a block before he remembered what he was doing out there and slowed to a walk.

Beaty sniffed the air and looked around with more care. Dozens of scents bombarded his nose from across the city. The smell of oils that leaked from the roads in the early morning sun was the strongest, but under that, he could smell baking bread. It would work if he couldn't find anything else, but he had learned some time ago that people who baked bread didn't throw it away in the morning.

He waited at a traffic stop and made sure to hang back from the humans who stood there. Several of them gave him dirty looks and he wasn't sure what would happen if he got too close. Still, none approached him while he maintained a wary distance.

On the tail of the crowd, Beaty crossed the road. A young woman waited for him to get across and leaned down with a hand held out toward him. He approached cautiously and sniffed tentatively. The ruffles on her sleeve had a strong floral perfume that almost made him sneeze. He was too nervous to draw any closer to her. Worried she would do something to him, he ran away. The woman straightened and waved a hand with a treat in it at his retreating back, but he did not slow down.

She called, "Wait! It's only a treat."

He didn't believe her and continued his journey. A little farther down the road, his nose twitched and took a big sniff of the breeze that came from the other side road. Fried food. Cooking meat. Perfect! He let his nose lead him in the direction of the promising aroma. Who could resist that? Certainly not *this* troll.

CHAPTER TWO

Beaty trotted up to the shop. A large crowd of people stood there —a group outside, and he saw even more inside through the window. He wasn't really all that good with specifics on counting, but it was enough to make things difficult. In a concerted effort to look pathetic, he lowered his head and slunk to the door.

A man shoved him back with a booted foot and stamped in his direction, waved his arms, and yelled, "Get!"

The troll-retriever darted toward the corner, his tail tucked between his legs. His side still ached from the kick earlier and he didn't want a repeat of that. Before he ducked out of sight, he noticed a man who stood beside the bully. This one seemed kinder and wore a tall yellow hat, and he smacked the shoulder of the man with the boot.

"Not cool, Jason." He shook his head and pushed inside the store.

Jason followed him in as he glared at his back. "How do you know my name? Who are you?"

"Ted Lancaster," he replied with a jaunty tip of his hat. "And your name tag is on your shirt."

The bully grumbled to himself and looked into the window display case.

Once safely behind the corner, Beaty waited for a few moments before he stuck his head tentatively around to survey the scene. He half hoped that everyone had forgotten about him. Maybe he could run fast enough to slip inside when one of them entered. Most of the people had turned back to their line but Jason looked directly at him. Well, glared at him, actually. The troll-retriever retreated and looked for a way to the back of the shop.

He had to go a few stores down to find the alley entrance and stopped to check the garbage bin on the way. It wasn't empty, but there wasn't anything in it that he would call *food* either. The alley led behind the row of shops, only one of which made food. From his new vantage point, he could smell the cooking even more strongly.

The rear of the building had an open window that leaned outward. The aromas rose from the open top and slid around the eaves and rooftop drain. A pipe from the drain ran vertically along the wall only a few feet from the open window and terminated behind another garbage bin. These people sure threw a lot of stuff away.

Beaty crossed to the refuse and returned to his true shape—barely five inches tall, but with a spike of green hair almost as big as he was. It would be a lot easier for him to get inside like this than as a dog. At least he hoped it would.

One of the lids of the garbage bin was slightly askew, the edge a little buckled so it no longer fit properly. He took a moment to check inside and identified mostly old garbage and a half-torn bag with rather unappealing goop leaking out of it. Nothing that smelled or looked edible, he realized regretfully. He vaulted from the bin, caught the drain pipe, and slid down a few inches before he gained purchase.

Holding tightly to the pipe, he scaled the side until he was level with the open window. He worked his way around to one of the support struts, leaned forward, and flung himself at his target. Beaty's arms windmilled and legs pumped the air for all he was worth to extend his clumsy flight. His momentum careened him into the edge of the window, chest first, and he flailed to get a good grip on it.

Unfortunately, the impact knocked him back and his hands scrabbled in vain as he slid and finally tumbled into empty space. He bounced off the drain pipe and directly into the partially open trash can, struck the open bag with a *thud,* and scattered garbage in all directions.

He shoved the refuse out of the way, found his feet, and held his arms on his sides to strike a *very* impressive pose. At least, he thought so. There wasn't anyone else around to tell him otherwise, so that was what he planned to keep believing.

A bubble gum wrapper fell across his face and he slapped at it, then tried to pull it away. It was stuck to something—gum, by the smell of it. After a few attempts, he managed to dislodge it but the gum itself was stuck in his hair and wouldn't move. He gave up on that and climbed out of the trash can.

A little disgruntled, he resumed his attempt and scrabbled up the pipe once more. Beaty climbed higher than before. He didn't stop until he was at the next strut above the one he'd used in his last disastrous attempt. This time, when he jumped, he cleared the edge of the window without a problem. Unfortunately, the damp glass was no easier for his feet to find a grip on than it had been for his hands.

He flailed his arms yet again as he skidded down the slanted window and tried to grab onto anything he could find but failed horribly. He rocketed off the edge of the glass and somehow managed to swing into the back room of the shop, where he bounced across the floor and finally stopped at the edge of a fridge. Luckily for him, none of the staff were in the back during his display of aerial acrobatics so he had a few moments to recover.

Beaty decided that moment would be a good time for a rest and promptly passed out.

CHAPTER THREE

A tabby cat startled awake as something bounced across the area she was in. She padded to the edge of the cabinet and peered across the back room of the shop. Something was definitely there. She should know, after all. This was her domain. The humans trusted her to protect them from vermin. Her eyes wide and ears twitching, she scanned the room. At first, she looked for motion, but when she found none, she looked for anything out of the norm. Anything that didn't belong.

She finally saw something laying on the ground, and it didn't seem to be moving. Stealthily, she padded along the top of the cabinet, hopped to the next one, and made her way to a position above the creature that had invaded her territory. Her scrutiny confirmed that it had still not moved. She still didn't know what it was. It was the wrong color, for one thing, and even from up there, she could tell it didn't smell right.

But she had a job to do. She dropped on the creature, pinned it to the ground, and snapped her head forward to bite it.

Beaty jerked awake when the cat landed on him and yanked his head to the side, his eyes wide in shock.

The cat barely missed, and he grabbed her face to hold her

head back. She jerked against his grasp, whipped her head back and forth, and pulled in an attempt to free herself.

The troll held on for dear life. He desperately wished he could turn into a dog or anything else larger than what he was now but was too focused on avoiding being eaten to manage it. The cat swatted repeatedly at him, but he was too close to her face for the blows to harness much force. She jumped and spun wildly. Beaty catapulted free to smack into a cabinet door. He rebounded and rolled to his feet.

The cat paced menacingly as he backed away, his hands out. He stumbled as his foot caught on a mat on the floor and the cat pounced. She swatted his hands aside and bit at his head.

Thankfully, he ducked at the last moment and she found a mouthful of hair and gum instead of biting his face. She jerked back and chewed rapidly in an attempt to remove the mess from her mouth. Lengths of green hair and old gum protruded from the sides. She yowled in distress as she swatted at her own face.

In a rush, Beaty dove under the nearest cabinet and scrambled to get out of sight. With the cat making that much noise, it was certain that someone would come to investigate.

He'd barely tucked his legs out of sight when the door to the back room burst open and a short, older woman rushed in. She scooped the cat up to pet it and cooed softly as she carried it into a side room. The animal, distressed though it was, tried to get out of her arms and it clawed at the cabinet where the troll had taken refuge. The lady had a good grip, however, and closed the door behind her as they disappeared from sight.

Beaty gave them a few minutes before he crawled out. He wiped off the layer of dust he'd gathered from under the cabinet as best as he could but frankly, there was a ton of it under there. The result was that he ended up pushing it around more than cleaning himself.

He pulled at each of the cabinets and checked inside. There was little in this room worth filching. It seemed to be where they stored their extra equipment for *making* food, not where they stored the food itself. He found pots and pans and a few bags of grain, but nothing he could carry with him that would be worth the effort.

A little disappointed, he approached the door the woman came through and listened. Bustling noises and people calling orders and joking filtered through. From this close, he could smell the food easily. It took only a moment to return to the form of a golden retriever. He nosed the door open, then slipped inside.

In what was obviously the kitchen, several busy people rushed around, each with their tasks. A tall man with a hairnet on his head danced between several pans and sang to music playing through headphones in his ears. A short, plump man rushed into the room to scoop up a to-go box of food and return to the front of the store. Beaty kept out of sight and waited.

The chef opened a fridge and retrieved a container of bacon, pulled it open, and set it on the counter. The troll's mouth watered at the sight. As soon as the man turned away toward the stove, he jumped for the counter. He snatched the whole bag of bacon and sprinted to the front of the store. There was no way he would make it through the back door as a dog, but if he was fast, he could make it out the front.

He burst into the shop itself, barreled out from behind the counter, and almost ran into the plump man. Without pause, he raced around him and dodged customers in headlong flight.

Jason saw him and grabbed the door, pulled it closed, and blocked his path. He kicked out at the fugitive came close.

Beaty skidded on the slick flooring as he dodged and bounced against the wall. His breath *whooshed* out on impact and he dropped the bag of bacon.

The bully lunged at him, but the troll-retriever was too fast and swerved past toward the door. Jason tried to release the door, but his hand wouldn't comply. When he stepped forward to direct another kick, it swung open enough to let Beaty out when he shoved hard and pushed it fully open as he squeezed through. Ted smiled, his expression smug below the yellow hat, and tucked something into his sleeve. The angry man's hand finally released the door. He snatched the bacon up and scooped it into the bag as best as he could.

His breathing heavy, Beaty darted away from the store and raced down the block. He was more than pissed. It irked him to think that he'd been so close, but now, he'd need to start from scratch. There was no way he would get back into that store.

Jason took the bag of bacon back to the counter and held it out to the proprietor who took it to throw it away.

The man with the yellow hat held a hand up. "Hey, if you're going to toss that out anyway, do you mind if I take it for my dogs at home?"

The plump man shrugged, dropped the bacon in a brown bag, and set it aside to give to Ted.

CHAPTER FOUR

Beaty sprinted down the road. He paid barely any attention to where he was going and simply focused on putting as much distance between himself and possible pursuit as he could. Unthinking, he ran into the street and halfway across before a car skidded to a stop a scant inch away. He yelped and almost barked but too startled to manage it, then ran on.

A few blocks later—or maybe a dozen blocks, he hadn't really paid attention—he slowed to a walk. Breathing deeply, he padded along, his heart still racing. He entered the next alley and sniffed at the garbage bin. It had something almost fresh inside, so he stood on his back legs and pushed at the lid. He managed to lever it up enough to jump in.

He dug around inside. Using his nose as a guide, he found a half-eaten sandwich. The rest of the smells were phantoms of things long gone, and the sandwich was too small to be of much value.

A sudden cramp clawed at Beaty's stomach and he doubled over. He could feel Sandy's hunger eating away at her. Fear at the sound of someone or something large moving around in the building followed. With it, her feeling of protectiveness for the puppies pushed alongside her desire to remain hidden. He scrambled to his feet, shoved the lid open, and vaulted out of the bin. He had run half the remaining block toward the building Sandy was in before the feeling of overwhelming fear subsided.

Sandy was hungry, but she wasn't as afraid anymore. The sense of that had passed. Beaty was torn. He wanted—almost *needed*—to get to Sandy and comfort her but without food, this entire trip was a waste.

Across the street from Beaty, Jason had gotten the attention of animal control.

"Then the dog came running out of the back. I have no idea how it even managed to get there. I wasn't 'bout to let it steal a bag of bacon after I blocked it from getting in the door in the first place."

The woman from animal control nodded and wrote in her notebook. She was fairly sure that nothing would come of this but at least the story, as unlikely as it was, was interesting. "Yes, sir, and how did the dog open the door from the back?"

"It was a push door. It kinda shoved it, but I held the front door so it couldn't get out there."

"But you said it got away."

The man shuffled his feet and glanced around. "Well, yeah, when I blocked its path it slipped and dropped the food. So I tried to catch it and I guess I held onto the door 'cause I pulled it open and the dog..."

His voice drifted off as he caught sight of Beaty standing stock still across the street. He pointed excitedly. "There! There it is right there."

He immediately ran across the street to chase the dog and left the woman staring after him. She didn't even try to follow. When she saw how quickly the animal was running, she climbed into her car to circle the block.

Beaty was startled when the man shouted and sprinted

toward him. He bolted back the other way, ran down the alley, and crossed to the next street over.

His pursuer followed and closed the distance a little with every step.

The troll-retriever turned into a parking lot and ducked between rows of closely packed cars. He aimed for those that were closest together, intending to lose the human when the man had to slow down. When he reached the back of the lot, he skidded though a small gap under a chain link fence.

The man collided into one of the cars as he tried to slide between them and bounced into the other. He hit it hard enough to set the alarm off and stumbled out from between them toward the fence. The hole was too small for him to fit through and the top of the links were covered in barbed wire. He grabbed the barrier and shook it as he yelled.

Beaty ran out of sight. He circled around the block to head back in Sandy's direction, hoping to stay out of sight of Jason. He had an ache in his side, but he could no longer tell if it was from Sandy or was something that had happened to him while he tried to escape. He was worried about her and started to feel weak from his own hunger.

CHAPTER FIVE

Ted reached the front of the line and looked through the display. He removed his tall yellow hat and wiped the sweat from his forehead. "I'll take two crawlers, a fried turkey leg, and that bag of bacon."

The store owner, still behind the counter, put his order together and rung it up. "That'll be thirteen fifty."

He shook his head. "Thanks, Greg, but I want to pay for the bacon, too."

Greg smiled and waved him off. "No, I was going to throw it away and I love dogs. Take it, I insist. I almost wish that critter got away with it in the first place."

With a faint smile, Ted nodded in agreement and paid for his food, then scooped the bag up. "I appreciate it."

He left the store and looked for somewhere private, munching on the crawler as he went. This was the first rain-free day he'd seen there in the last week and he was glad to be out in the open. He replaced his yellow hat on his head and made sure to tuck his pointed ears under the brim as he did so. Thankfully, no one had noticed—or, at least, no one commented—when he removed it in the store. Then again, this was San Francisco, so pointed ears were likely the least weird thing most of them would see that day.

Ted found an out of the way nook in a parking lot behind some cars and a large panel truck. He set the bag of bacon down, wiped his hands off, and drew a wand from his pants pocket. He was proud of those pants, having tailored them himself to fit the wand sheath inside the pocket without disturbing the lines of the garment.

Holding the image of the emaciated, scared golden retriever in his mind, he drew patterns in the air with his wand. It left a faint tracery of light that only he could see that formed into an outline of the nearby streets—much like Google Maps, but made of magic and light. Ted was particularly proud of this spell.

He focused and allowed the magic to take hold and move the wand where it needed to go. His view of the world around him faded and the lines in his sight grew clearer. He felt the magic flow through his body and into the wand. The spell crystallized and became almost more real than the world around him.

A faint pulsing dot formed in the pattern. It drifted along the lines of the map and circled in on a road only a few blocks away. When it settled to a stop, Ted pushed the wand into the dot and flicked it. The map vanished and left a line of light as the dot rocketed to the left. He scooped the food up and hurried after the magical tracker.

Beaty leaned against the wall where he'd stopped. He was tired from all the frenetic activity and wasn't sure where to go next. The only thing he wanted more than to go to Sandy was to find enough food for her. His own stomach was woefully empty but at that moment, he couldn't tell the difference between that and what he sensed from his furry charge.

His ears perked up as he heard someone running in his direction.

He bolted away from the building. He'd almost made it back, but he had no intention of leading people to her. His flight took him between several cars stopped at the light and into a park. Beaty skidded in the mud and slid into a bush, where he dropped flat to the ground to wait. His fear was that Jason had caught up to him, certain that he was somehow still in pursuit and that he'd find him.

Ted slowed to a walk as he crossed the street. He felt bad that he'd startled the dog and didn't want to do it again. His line of light led him into the park and floated above a small copse of bushes, where it formed a faint circular pattern in the air. A puddle of mud in front of it showed crisscrossing paths where children had played in it over the last few days and a few dog prints.

Slowing further, he walked to the edge of the mud, knelt, and held the turkey leg out. "Here, puppy. I have some delicious food for you."

He waved the leg around almost as if he tried to fan the air with it and felt slightly silly.

Beaty watched as the man who'd defended him from Jason knelt in the mud. He was nervous and so remained crouched under the bush, unwilling to move. Despite the temptation, he couldn't quite believe that Ted would give him food. It had to be a trick...but Sandy was so hungry.

A wet stain spread up Ted's leg from where he knelt. "Well, crap, that'll be a pain to clean. Heeere, puppy."

The troll-retriever crawled to the edge of the bush and sniffed the air. He was careful to remain out of sight, but his visitor didn't seem to need to see him to know he was there. The smell of the turkey leg wafted temptingly, along with the bacon in the bag at the man's side. He pushed his head out of the bush.

Ted smiled and leaned forward, holding the turkey leg toward the animal as he left the bush.

Beaty froze when Ted moved, so the man froze too. He only moved the turkey leg and waved it gently in the dog's direction.

The retriever's stomach growled loudly enough that Ted could hear it clearly from where he knelt. He waited patiently, his arm extended until the dog stood and approached warily.

He covered the last few feet in a rush and snatched the food out of Ted's hand, half afraid the man would hold onto it and stop him from leaving.

Ted released the leg and tried to remain completely still otherwise, not wanting to startle the dog further.

Beaty slid in the mud but kept his feet and ran for the exit of the park.

"Wait!" The man scrambled to his feet and held the bag of bacon out. "This is for you too."

He was shocked enough to drop the bag when the dog skidded to a stop and ran back toward him.

Beaty scooped the bacon up, barely managing to keep the turkey leg in his mouth, and raced away.

CHAPTER SEVEN

Being careful not to drop or swallow his precious cargo, Beaty hurtled from the park by the most direct route he could find. Unfortunately, that meant he exited on the wrong side of it. He circled until he found his original path and tracked back along it.

He glanced constantly over his shoulder, still worried that Ted would follow him or that Jason would find him. It was hard for him to understand what had happened, and while it wasn't what he was used to, it felt...nice.

The food smelled so good that it made his stomach ache. He couldn't help but salivate as he ran to the alley that would take him to Sandy. Still, he held back and didn't eat any of it.

He hopped onto the bin, up to the rusted roof, and crawled through the hole in the wall. His mouth full of delicious food, he trotted over to where he'd left Sandy and the puppies.

The crumbled wall was broken! Pieces of it lay strewn about and Sandy and the puppies were gone.

Beaty dropped the food in shock. He was overwhelmed with a sudden sinking feeling and horror that he should have come back faster. No matter what, he should have been there when Sandy was scared and should have been here for the puppies and for her. The pain must have been her being attacked and injured by someone who slipped in while he was away. He knew he shouldn't have trusted anyone—he had been gone too long.

Something nudged his back leg and he almost hurdled over what remained of the wall. He spun and saw Bounder licking at the turkey leg.

Grinning, he scooped the food up and pushed Bounder with his nose. The rascal led him across the room and his tail wagged happily as he took him to where Sandy and the other puppies were. They'd moved to a more hidden area, out of sight of whoever had been in there before.

He dropped the bacon in front of the puppies. They promptly tore the bag apart and licked and bit at the delicious smelling meat. That gave him time to set the turkey leg down beside Sandy and return to his troll form.

A huge grin on his face, he tore little chunks of turkey off and fed them to her and took only the smallest nibble himself. They were his family, and that was all that mattered.

AUTHOR NOTES

What a wild ride. From the first moment I picked up *Death Becomes Her* until I wrote a few (too many? You be the judge) short stories in the Kurtherian Gambit Fan's Write to joining the moderating team and going to Vegas. Meeting and working with Sarah, Nat, and Erika. It's all been amazing. I can honestly say that my life has changed for the better, all starting with one little book written by Michael Anderle. Thank you for reading this short story. I hope you enjoyed it and all the other stories fans submitted for this. We write because you read.

HERKIMER HEIST

BY LISA FRETT

Stephanie and Trig are called to solve a case of stolen, very expensive, magical crystals that were taken from Witches in central New York.

It might not be as exciting as saving drunken Ogres from the mountains of Vermont, but at least saving drunk Ogres doesn't get you turned into poultry.

Follow the continued exploits of Stephanie and Trig as they try to keep magic hidden from humans on Earth.

PROLOGUE

It was a beautiful afternoon. Aaron and his family took advantage of the clear skies and cool fall weather. They couldn't pass up the chance for a walk through their neighborhood.

Their street was lined with trees wearing leaves of bright yellows, brilliant oranges, and bright cherry-reds. There was nothing more beautiful and vibrant than New York's Mohawk valley in the fall.

As the family neared an intersection, a vehicle's tires screeched as it sped nearby. They looked up, startled, when a black pickup truck careened into view.

The vehicle entered the intersection, jackknifed, and spun into a sweeping slide. The driver lost control and the momentum hurled the truck onto the curb. Aaron's wife and their three-year-old daughter were directly in its path. He tried to push them out of the way but was too slow. The truck struck his wife and little girl.

The vehicle roared away from the scene of the accident. Aaron's only child died on impact and his wife died later at the hospital. In one impossible, crazy second, he felt his whole life was destroyed.

For several months, he remained isolated from the rest of the world. Aaron's universe died on an intersection in central New York State.

Other than the grieving man, there were no witnesses to the hit and run accident. The police had no leads and their case grew cold. It was placed with the myriad of other cases that went unsolved. He even hired a private investigator whose investigation also came up empty.

With nowhere else to turn, Aaron spoke to an aunt of his, one who had a secret only known to a few people in the family. His Aunt Helene was a witch from an odd-sounding place called Oriceran.

He met her at a local restaurant and hugged her in greeting. "It's good to see you again, Helene."

"I'm always glad to have you visit but I wish it was for happier reasons." She motioned for her nephew to sit at their table. "I'll do what I can to find this guy for you. I know of a spell that can help."

He looked at her with the full weight of desperation behind the tears that pooled in his eyes. "I can't thank you enough, Helene. I need closure. I'll do whatever I can to get it."

Helene took his hands in hers. "It's okay, dear. Where I'm from, family takes care of family." She smiled warmly at him, which put him at ease.

His aunt explained to him that she would need four very specially charged Herkimer diamond crystals for a location spell. "I know a certain individual who is good at acquiring objects like this. He isn't cheap, but he'll get what we need."

They worked out the details of their plan and Aaron made certain that the funds were available for Helene's supplier.

Once the preliminary details were worked out, the two were able to settle down to a pleasant meal.

CHAPTER ONE

Trig opened his eyes from a deep sleep and bellowed an earth-shattering, "What the fuck!"

He scrambled out of bed and grabbed his alarm clock. It was the first thing he saw that would work as an impromptu weapon. He yanked the plug out of the outlet and threw the clock at a huge spider that sat on the bed directly beside where his head had been a scant second before.

Across the bed from him, Stephanie—the love of his life—doubled over and laughed uncontrollably. She carefully lifted the offending arachnid from their bed. Giggling she said, "It's only rubber, silly." She held it up to his face and shook it. "See. It's fake."

Her grin remained widened as she set it on the nightstand. Looking at Trig, Stephanie sucked in a breath. *He's stunning. And as totally naked as the day he was born.* Too bad she was already showered and dressed for the day. She smiled mischievously.

He walked up to her and put his arms around her waist. Pulling her into him, he kissed her lips gently. When he came up for breath, he said softly, "You know I hate spiders."

With her arms around his neck, she replied, "That's what

makes it funny, silly. Besides, I had to get you back for that time you put the skunk in my car."

He laughed. "In my defense, the person who loaned it to me promised that its scent glands were removed."

"Oh, its glands were removed all right. But it made a mess that took the detailers forever to clean."

"Yeah. Okay. Bad on my part." He kissed her forehead lightly and smiled as he looked into her eyes. "But I would never knowingly do anything to hurt you." He leaned to kiss her lips.

Stephanie found it difficult to pull away. Swallowing hard, she said in a low voice, "I think we should get ready for work."

"I think we should call in late," was Trig's husky response.

She was almost ready to agree with him when, as if on cue, her phone rang. With a heavy sigh, she retrieved it and frowned at the screen when she saw it was their boss.

Reluctantly, she pulled out of her partner's embrace. "Hi, Captain, what's up?"

Trig sighed. He turned toward the bathroom so he could take a quick, somewhat cool shower to get ready for work.

"I have a case for you. It's across the lake in New York—Herkimer, to be exact." Captain Bartholomew Rothseth, head of the Vermont office of the Order of the Silver Griffins answered. "Rather than coming into the office today, I need you to grab your go-bags and head there directly."

Stephanie thought this was odd. "Herkimer has a large magic presence because of its crystal deposits. They have a local Griffin office. Can't they handle it? I mean, I have no problem going there for a job but honestly, I'm confused."

"That's understandable. The Herkimer office asked for assistance. They're currently over-tasked and need a couple of extra hands."

"What do they have for us?" Stephanie asked.

"I'll send the information to your tablets." She could hear the captain typing on his keyboard. "There. You should have the files now."

"Trig and I will look them over and head out." She glanced at her tablet and saw the folder labeled, **Herkimer**.

"Great. Thanks, Steph. If you need anything from me, let me know. Chief Yordan is the head of the Herkimer office. I'll let him know to expect the two of you. If it turns out you need a place to stay, they'll set you up." As an afterthought, he told her, "Tell Trig hi from me."

"Will do, boss. Talk to you later." With that, she hung up.

Trig stepped out of the bathroom, towel-drying his hair. "What's up?" he asked.

"Herkimer asked for help with a case. The boss wants us to head that way." She handed him his tablet and they walked into their living room where they sat to read through the files.

"Hmmm... Theft of crystals." Trig looked at Stephanie and asked, "Will you be okay with this?" His concern stemmed from a recent case where a crystal was used to drain her of her magical energy. It had almost killed her.

She threw one of the pillows from the sofa at him. "Of course I'll be all right. I'm a professional, if nothing else. I'll merely make certain I have a couple of extra mundane weapons with me." She paused. "You know, in case a crystal sucks me dry again." The memory made her shiver.

Trig saw that she was making light of it, so he relaxed. "Okay then. We have theft of crystals, Herkimer diamond crystals to be exact. Let's see...there are no witnesses, nothing seen on video, and no evidence found at the scenes." He smiled as he looked up at Stephanie. "I always like a good challenge."

CHAPTER TWO

Lodd pulled the hood over his head. It was late at night and dressed all in black, the short Elf took advantage of the darkness. He moved furtively using the shadows to cloak him and made his way through the town.

He had been very lucky so far. He was hired to 'acquire' four charged Herkimer diamond crystals from local witches. The buyer wanted them for some kind of spell.

Crystals from Herkimer County were some of the most powerful in the world and were well-known for their metaphysical properties. They could store, focus, amplify, and transfer energy. Many believed they could act as conduits for life forces, and magical beings from Oriceran were drawn to their power. Because of this, many Oricerans on Earth lived in the Herkimer region of central New York.

The elf stood outside the building where his final target was located and checked his gear. Once he was certain that everything was in place, he set to work. He was really good at remaining silent and hidden and also had a butt-load of gadgets with him. It was these talents and toys that made him very good at acquiring items that people didn't want to part with.

One of his favorite sets of toys was gloves and shoes with retractable spikes. The prongs were sharp enough and strong enough to enable him to climb buildings such as the brick one before him. Lodd activated the spikes and began his ascent.

He had reached the second story when he noticed an open window in the building across the alley. The sight of a man bathing in a tub filled with bubbles drew a short laugh from the burglar. The elf removed one of his climbing gloves and retrieved his cell phone from a pouch. He snapped a picture of the contented bather. After adding the text, **Oooh... Bubbles...** to the image, he posted it to social media. His grin wide, he returned his phone to the pouch, donned his glove carefully, and continued.

Lodd made it to the window of the room where the crystal was located, and he pulled out a round disk. He peeled paper from one side of it and stuck it on the window. Both the object and the glass around it slowly faded but removed only enough window glass for him to fit through. He eased himself through the hole and landed on the carpeted floor with a *thump*. Apparently, he was graceful in all things except landings.

Cautiously, he stood and studied his surroundings. It was dark, so he couldn't really see very well. From a little pouch attached to his belt, the elf withdrew a marble-sized sphere that emitted a soft, pale blue glow. It illuminated the area around him sufficiently for him to be able to find what he was looking for.

In one of the corners of the room, the dim lighting revealed an ornate box with a set of four small images carved on it. The images depicted a bird, a tree, a flower, and a snake. "Hmmm..." Lodd considered the symbols and their implications. "Magically sealed and possibly trapped."

He was certain that he could open it, but he hoped that the witch who owned the box kept her passwords written down somewhere like most people did.

His logical first step was to check the desk drawers, but he was unable to find anything. Next, he bent and peered underneath the desk. Sure enough, a yellow sticky note was stuck to the underside.

He pulled it from the desk and looked at it. The letters **F-S-B-T** were written on it. He walked over to the box and studied the images carefully. "They could have at least tried to make it a little more challenging," he whispered and shrugged.

Lodd pressed the magical images in the sequence defined on the paper—the flower, the snake, the bird, and finally, the tree. A line sizzled and smoked along the top edges. Once the sizzling stopped, he removed the top of the box and set it on the floor.

A clear crystal rod with a point at each end rested on a little pillow. After a careful examination of the cushioning, Lodd identified a little pressure switch. He withdrew a small rock from his pouch, put one finger carefully on the switch, and removed the crystal. His finger still resting on the switch, he slid his prize into a hidden pocket on his shirt with his free hand.

The crystal secured, he placed the rock over his finger, held his breath, and pressed down on the stone while he slid his finger off the switch. He exhaled a long breath once he realized that he hadn't tripped any alarms or traps.

The elf replaced the top of the box with slow caution and pressed the images in sequence. He rather liked the way the lid sealed itself effectively.

Lodd patted his shirt where the crystal was and contemplated the money he would make from its sale. His buyer should be very happy with this purchase.

With that thought in mind, he dowsed the light of his sphere and slid out through the hole in the window. Once outside, he removed a different disk from his pouch and held it in front of the hole. A glasslike substance formed from the disk to seal his point of entry. It wasn't as strong and durable as the original glass, but it should hide the fact that anyone was there—at least long enough for him to get away.

CHAPTER THREE

On the way to Herkimer, Trig took his turn at the wheel once they'd filled up with gas, while Stephanie reviewed the reports related to their case.

"We're obviously dealing with someone from Oriceran, or someone who knows about Oriceran. The containers these crystals were in were all magically sealed and each of the missing crystals were magically cleansed and charged Herkimer diamonds."

She paused in her reading and took a moment to look out at the passing landscape. "I love driving through the Adirondacks. They are so beautiful."

Trig looked at her from the corner of his eyes and smiled. "Yes, they are."

Stephanie returned the smile and turned back to the files. Thinking of motive, she said, "These crystals are all very expensive, but they are also very powerful for magical beings. So, is the thief a magical working for himself and looking for power? Or is he doing it for the money?"

He looked thoughtfully toward the road. "Hmm... The first

theft happened a little over a month ago, and that crystal hasn't shown up anywhere yet. How far did the Herkimer agents get?"

"Not very far. The local office has been checking known fences. I think they even checked the black market on Oriceran a couple of times. Nothing matching the descriptions of any of the missing crystals has shown up."

A light rain set in, so Trig rolled the sedan windows up and turned the vehicle's fan on. "It looks more like someone wants them for their magical properties. It makes sense and is the only reason I can think of that these crystals haven't shown up in any market."

"Maybe. Or maybe someone has stolen them for a specific buyer?" She closed the files and turned the tablet off.

"Hm. That could be. Let's check in at the office and then we'll visit the crime scenes ourselves. We'll do better once we have a firsthand view."

They made it to the Herkimer office of the Order of the Silver Griffins and met Chief Yordan. He was a stately Light Elf and also Captain Rothselth's boss. Technically, that made him their boss as well, but not directly.

The chief had given them a rundown of what he knew about the thefts. Unfortunately, the order agents who were assigned to the previous cases were busy elsewhere. That was why Stephanie and Trig were called in to help.

The chief showed the two to a couple of empty desks. "You can use these desks and computers. Let me know if you need anything else."

They thanked him and settled down to work. Stephanie and Trig made arrangements to visit the theft locations. During each call, the victims were very accommodating and happy to know that their cases were still open and under investigation.

As they were leaving the office, Chief Yordan stopped them.

"Guys, hold up a minute."

"What's up, Chief?" she asked.

"I've just had another case come in. I've sent the address and what information we have to your tablets."

"Thanks, Chief," Trig said. "Let's go." He held the door open for his partner.

Stephanie and Trig were met by the victim as they arrived at the scene.

"Phew! I'm so glad you're here." A middle-aged woman shook each of their hands. "Name's Janelle." She hurried them into the building. "I'm the witch who owns this place."

As they walked up several flights of stairs, she told them, "I guess I'm paranoid, and apparently for good reason. I check my lockbox every morning after I arrive."

They reached an office door and she opened it for them to enter. "I also check it every night before leaving for the day. That's how I know that the crystal was there when I left at 4:00 PM yesterday."

This woman's a force of nature, Stephanie thought. She wished she had her energy.

Janelle continued as she showed them the box. "When I checked this morning, there was a rock in its place."

Stephanie was recording as Janelle was speaking. She asked, "What time did you arrive this morning?"

"I came in around 7:00 and checked the lockbox shortly after." The witch sat in her chair and wrung her hands nervously.

Trig put a hand on her shoulder. "Can you tell if anything is out of place? Is there anything else missing?"

Still seated, Janelle looked around carefully. "No to both questions. At least not that I can see." Continuing to look around,

Janelle put up a hand. "Wait." She reached down for a yellow sticky note on the floor. It was the paper that had the passcode clue for the lockbox. She slumped in her chair. "I think I know how they managed to unlock my lockbox." She handed the paper to Trig.

Shaking her head, she said, "I feel so stupid right now."

He took the paper and tried to comfort her. "There's no reason to feel that way. It happens more often than you'd expect. It's difficult trying to remember your passwords and codes.

With a wry shrug, she said, "Yes, well, I'm a witch. I should have known better. I could have at least put an invisibility spell or some something like it on the notelet."

Trig nodded. "It's a good idea for the future. Right now, let's get your crystal back."

He glanced at the clue and asked, "Where is this normally kept?"

Janelle pointed at her desk. "Under there." Raising her hands in a gesture of frustration, she said, "I'm always afraid I'll forget it."

The forensic technician who had arrived on scene didn't wait for the agents to ask. He opened his fingerprint kit and set to work on the desk.

As she examined the office, Stephanie thought aloud. "I wonder how they got in. The only access points are the door and window. She turned to Janelle and asked, "Was the door locked when you came in this morning?"

The witch nodded. "Yes."

Stephanie looked closely at the door and its frame. "There's no sign of forced entry."

Trig looked out the window at the structure across the alley. "We should see if there are any cameras pointing at this building."

He took a closer look at the apartments opposite and realized that something bothered him—the scene somehow looked familiar. When he retrieved his phone to take a picture of what he saw, the device opened to a social media app that he had used earlier. Sure enough, there was a meme posted to a page he frequented. Whether it was simply coincidence or luck, he didn't care, but the image on the phone was of the same window and included a man bathing in a tub with the caption, **Oooh... Bubbles...** Trig couldn't believe it. He actually looked right at the real thing—sans man bathing, of course.

He had to smile. "Got ya! What are the chances of this ever happening?"

Stephanie looked at him. "What do you mean? What do you got?"

"Come look at this." Trig motioned her over to him. "Someone posted this meme last night. I remembered seeing this earlier. While you were driving, I checked social media." He pointed out the window to the alley and held out the phone as he grinned broadly. "Look closely at the picture."

Stephanie smiled. Sure enough, the image in the meme was of the window across the alley.

After leaving Janelle's office, they wanted to inspect the exterior of the building. Standing in the alley, Stephanie looked up at the third-floor window. "I don't suppose you know of a flying spell?"

Trig laughed at his partner. "I'm afraid not."

"Well, a woman can only hope." She shielded her eyes against the glare and squinted upward. "Since we're most likely dealing with an Oriceran, I want to rule out that the perp entered through the third story window."

"You're thinking magic?" he asked.

She nodded. "Yep." Turning to him, she asked, "Rappelling gear, then?"

He smiled. "We just happen to have some in the trunk."

Stephanie gave him a quizzical look. "No shit? Really?"

"Really. Remember that huge Ogre? Bulferd, I think his name was. He got drunk and fell down the mountain near Jay?"

"Ugh." She grimaced. Yes. That dude was the size of an elephant. Nobody had a feather spell with enough distance to reach him, so I had to rappel. I landed on his stomach and he let out the loudest, and smelliest, belch I have ever experienced." She shivered as she thought back to that incident. "It started a small avalanche. I had to hide behind him so I wasn't pelted by rocks. Then he had to go and fart! *Ugh!* That was disgusting!"

Trig laughed. "I noticed that you didn't try to save him from the falling rocks."

Stephanie laughed. "He was never in any danger. They bounced right off him."

"Yes, well, we never took the gear out of the car. I left it in the trunk and thought that it might come in handy someday. You never know when a drunken Ogre might fall down a mountain."

She smacked his arm and turned her attention to the roof. "Well, I guess I'll grab the gear and head on up."

When she had retrieved what she needed and gone inside to use the stairs to the roof, Stephanie set her anchors up and put her equipment on.

At the edge of the roof, she looked down and scowled. *Ugh. I hate this part.* She made a final check that everything was secure, turned, and leaned back into her harness.

Stephanie unhooked her personal anchor, hollered, "Rappel on," and began her decent.

Once safely at the third-story window, she yelled to her partner, "You know, it would have been so much safer to simply rent a lift."

Trig smiled as he responded, "Maybe. But I know you. This is much more fun." As an afterthought, he added, "And it's much cheaper."

He couldn't see it, but she gave him the finger.

From the outside, the window looked different. She peered at a slight abnormality that wasn't visible from the interior. In the shape of a circle, it seemed large enough for a small person to slip through.

Stephanie unhooked a camera attached to her harness and took a picture of the glass, hoping that the abnormality would be visible. A closer inspection revealed scratches that ended at the edge of the irregularity.

She twisted to look across the alley. From her vantage point, she could tell that the image in the meme that Trig showed her was taken from a little lower. She descended to the correct height, where she had a clear view of the bathtub—and the man who entered the bathroom at that precise moment. He had a good view of her too. She couldn't hear what he said, but he was very animated and appeared to be yelling at her.

In response, she simply waved at him. *It's not my fault he doesn't use curtains.* She turned to examine the building as she inched downward.

A careful study of the wall revealed very small holes in the brick. She made her hand into a claw shape and compared it to the marks. Sure enough, it looked like they were made by hands. The culprit obviously had some kind of thin blades attached to the tips of the digits. Stephanie took pictures of the punctures and others with her hands in front of them.

When she landed on the ground, she explained to Trig what she had found.

"So," her partner began, "we have a magical someone who can climb the side of buildings, somehow change the properties of glass so that they can climb through the window, and are able to repair the window on the way out."

"And they are at least an individual of average height, judging by the size of the window distortion," Stephanie added.

He held a hand up. "If that is how the individual got into the building."

"I don't know, Trig. I think this is exactly how our perpetrator entered and exited the office. We have the internet photo. There is the lack of any signs of forced entry. There are the holes in the wall that appear to have been made by claw-shaped hands. I feel good about this."

"Okay, then." His nod was businesslike. "We'll use this as our current working theory."

Stephanie made an observation as she stowed the rappelling gear. "The chief must have notified the local police of our presence." She looked at the window across the alley. "I can't believe that the man in the bathroom didn't call them."

Trig looked at her, bemused. "He was there?"

She nodded and smiled. "Oh yeah. You should have seen him. He jumped around in his bathrobe and yelled at me. I don't know what he said, but I'm sure it wasn't good."

"I wish I could have seen that." He grinned.

Once everything was put away, they headed back to the office to go over what they had learned thus far.

CHAPTER FOUR

The partners sat at the desk of one of the computer forensic technicians. "It's funny, you know?" Stephanie said.

"What's funny?" Trig asked.

"Here we are, in an office filled with some of the most powerful magic users on Earth, and we still have to rely heavily on mundane investigative methods."

"Well, that's because magic users are still making some mundane mistakes." He grinned at her. "I like not having to rely on magic for everything. It can become a crutch."

She turned to the technician. "Do you have anything yet?"

He looked up and smiled. "I do. And it's not mundane. The account associated with our picture belongs to an Elf named Lodd."

The chief, seated at a nearby desk, overheard what was said. "Lodd, huh? As soon as you mentioned a meme, I thought it might be him. He's well known around here. He's a burglar, and a very good one too. But he likes to take pictures of random things near his heists and post them as memes. It's like a calling card for him."

"He always ends up getting caught," the technician added.

Chief Yordan chuckled dryly. "I think he likes getting caught. It's why he does it."

Trig had a questioning look on his face. "He likes getting caught?"

"Yeah. But he's always able to escape before reaching lockup," the chief explained.

"You don't seem too upset over it, Chief." Stephanie observed.

"Nope. As I said, he always gets caught. And we eventually get the items back. He doesn't hurt anyone and doesn't damage property. As long as we can return the items to their original owners, I don't stress too much over his antics. So far, once the items are returned, the victims don't usually want the hassle of pressing charges."

Chief Yordan stopped as if struck by a new thought. "I think it's a game for him. But occasionally, he works on commission. This time, I think it be the case. He's been very specific about the items he's taken."

"Do we have any idea where he is now?" Trig asked.

"No. But we're familiar with most of his aliases. We'll investigate them and let you know when we find him." The chief turned to the technician. "Mike, upload a picture of Lodd for the agents."

"Done, sir. I sent it to their tablets."

"Thanks, Mike." Trig said as he turned to Stephanie. "I saw a pizza place nearby. What do you say we pay them a visit?"

She smiled at him. "You know me so well. Let's eat!"

CHAPTER FIVE

Lodd had the four crystals that the buyer requested packed and ready to move. They were each wrapped in cloth and placed in a backpack for easy transport. He checked the intrusion detectors that he had set up around his hotel room and none of them were tripped. *That's good. They haven't found me yet.*

The local Silver Griffins knew him well and he knew that they would eventually find him. But for Lodd, it really was a game. He liked the challenge of escaping once caught. This time, though, he had to get the items to his customer first. Once they were safely delivered, he could think about the fun of the chase.

Chief Yordan was able to track the elf's movements to a hotel room just inside the city. He currently used an old alias. It was old enough that the Griffin commander assumed that Lodd might have thought the order had forgotten it. That same alias was also traced to a vehicle that was parked at the hotel. Once the information was known, the chief passed it on to Trig and Stephanie.

Both agents wanted to be certain that the person in the hotel was, in fact, the elf in question. Trig found a fly nearby and waved his wand at it, and a few sparks struck the insect. It wobbled and buzzed a few times before it came to what appeared to be attention.

Trig stared into the fly's thousands of eyes for a moment. He then pointed his wand toward the hotel room and the insect immediately flew away.

"Can you see what the fly sees?" Stephanie asked him.

"Kind of. It's really confusing, though. It's like thousands of pictures put together to form one image." He wore a look of extreme concentration.

"Like a photographic mosaic?"

"Yeah. It's like that. Only when it moves, it gives me motion sickness. It's really weird." He looked more at ease as the fly came to a stop. "And now, I am the proverbial 'fly on the wall.'"

"Only not so proverbial," she observed.

Trig soon confirmed that the individual in the room was the Elf they pursued. The thief wrapped a crystal in some fabric to make the last of four wrapped bundles.

"This looks like our elf. There appear to be four crystals. He wrapped them in cloth and placed them in a backpack."

He cut his connection to the fly.

Now much less green in the face, he turned to Stephanie. "He might be getting ready to make the sale."

She nodded at her partner as she knelt to put a tracer under Lodd's tiny Smart Fortwo car.

"Well, we know he doesn't feel the need to compensate for anything," she commented with a laugh.

Trig raised his eyebrows. "Should I be worried?"

Stephanie smiled and winked at him. "Hell no."

"Wait. Why did you wink?" He knew that he shouldn't worry, but for some reason, that wink made him do exactly that. With a sigh, he thought that life was much less complicated without a girlfriend. Then, he smiled and reminded himself that life was so much better and more fun with one.

"Let's get back to our car and wait. I have the stakeout coffee and snacks all set up," Trig said as he headed to their sedan. They made themselves comfortable as they waited for something to happen.

It took a couple of hours and darkness had all but settled in before Lodd left his room. He had the backpack with him and glanced around furtively before he got into his car. Her partner dozed in the passenger seat, so she nudged him awake. "Hey, sleepyhead, he's on the move."

Trig straightened and buckled his seat belt. Stephanie followed the elf at a safe distance. The tracker worked well, so they were able to remain far enough behind where they wouldn't be seen.

"That really is a cute little car." He laughed. "It reminds me of those little toy cars you'd get from the dollar store. You know, the ones with the wheels that pop on and off?"

"Ha-ha. Okay. I guess I can see that." As an afterthought, she added, "I bet it has great gas consumption, though."

"True. But I don't think I'd want to drive something that small in any traffic. A fender bender would total that car."

He frowned at the tracker. "He stopped."

Stephanie turned the sedan's lights off as she eased closer to Lodd's car. Their sedan was a dark enough color that, when in shadows at night, it was practically impossible to see. The building their quarry had pulled up to was very well-lit, though.

The Elf spoke with a man and a woman. The man handed him some money and Lodd handed the bag over to the woman.

Stephanie took pictures of the three people and called the office.

"Hi, Chief. I'm sending you pictures of three individuals. One is Lodd, and we suspect the other two are the buyers. They already made the hand-off."

"Good work. Bring them in." He paused. "Unfortunately, I don't have any agents to send as backup."

"It's okay, Chief. Trig and I have this." She ended the call and smiled broadly at her partner. "Let's go get us some thieves."

The two exited their vehicle and approached the suspects quietly. When they were close enough, they pointed their wands at the trio. Trig hollered, "Freeze! By order of the order!"

Stephanie looked at him. "Really? Order of the order?"

He shrugged. "It sounded good in my mind."

The woman raised a wand quickly and pointed it at him. She mumbled a couple of words and *poof,* Trig turned into a chicken.

"Hey!" Stephanie yelled. "That's my cock!" *That would totally be hilarious if my partner-slash-boyfriend hadn't turned into a cock...er...a chicken.*

She aimed her wand at the witch and a bolt of electricity erupted to strike her target in the shoulder. The backpack that contained the crystals fell.

The man yelled, "Aunt Helene!"

She yelled, "Run Aaron!"

Stephanie then directed her wand at the woman's head and released a concussive bolt. The missile struck her in the forehead, and she tumbled. Helene tried a few times to stand but the force of the bolt had obviously addled her brain. Whenever she made the attempt, her head would wobble, and she'd fall once again. Each time she collapsed, the Trig-chicken would peck at her face.

Between her confused state and the chicken, she wasn't going anywhere.

Lodd took advantage of the initial confusion and ran. He made it to his car, and he sped away.

Aaron didn't know what to do. He turned toward the female agent and launched himself to tackle her. They landed in a tangle of limbs.

Stephanie was able to turn on her side, crunch up, and push out from him.

She scrambled to her feet and assumed a fighting stance. Aaron looked at her and, when he realized that he didn't stand a chance against her, he ran.

The chicken clearly had Helene under control, so Stephanie sprinted in pursuit of the fleeing man.

The warehouse was located between various businesses. Aaron ran into the alley behind them and hesitated when he passed piles of boxes on pallets. He shoved the crates into Stephanie's path. She managed to dodge a couple but the last of them were in her way and she slowed a little to hurdle over them.

Aaron reached a dead end where a dog was chained to a heavy pipe. The animal barked angrily at him. He froze for a moment but soon decided that he feared the dog more than the witch and turned to run back the way he came.

Stephanie was close and he ducked instinctively behind a dumpster. He waited until she was close enough and pushed the heavy trash container into her.

"Ow! Fuck! You asshole, that hurt!" she exclaimed as she spun to continue the chase. Aaron now headed back out of the alley.

Without slowing, Stephanie raised her wand and aimed at him, center mass. The shot missed and struck the brick wall immediately ahead of him. Debris from the strike battered his side but he continued his headlong flight.

Aaron reached the warehouse where the chase had begun. He glanced over his shoulder at her and tripped over a chicken that ran into his path.

"Squawk!" The feathered nuisance sounded almost triumphant when the man fell. His rapid tumble stopped when his face struck the pavement.

Stephanie cringed. "That had to hurt." She crouched and put handcuffs on him before she turned to the chicken. "Honey…"

She smiled. "I have the hardest time trying not to repeat any cock jokes right now."

Trig squawked again as he ran in haphazard circles and flapped his wings indignantly.

She hauled Aaron to his feet, and they walked to where the witch Helene still sat dazed and immobile.

"I must have overdone that concussive spell," Stephanie said and glanced at Trig. "She turned you into a chicken. I was so pissed at that."

"Squawk."

The witch made offered no resistance when she turned her over and put her second set of cuffs on her. Stephanie poured a couple drops of a light healing potion into Helene's mouth. It was enough to bring her to her senses.

"Well, hello there. I'm glad you can come back to us. I need you to change my partner back into a wizard. He's a cute chicken, but he's a better agent as a wizard."

Helene nodded. "Please... My wand? I won't run. I didn't mean to harm anyone. I only tried to help my nephew. Please... I'll turn him back."

Stephanie nodded. "Know that if you try anything, I will put you down harder next time." She went to the sedan and retrieved a couple of nylon twist ties and secured Helen's ankles.

"I want to trust you, but you'll understand if I err on the side of caution," she said as she tightened the restraints.

She freed Helene's hands from the handcuffs but stood ready in case the witch decided to attack or run instead of reversing the spell.

The woman pointed the wand at Trig, mumbled a few words, and *poof,* he was a wizard once more.

Stephanie didn't understand the technicalities behind some spells, but she was very grateful that he changed back fully clothed.

Her partner restored, she put the handcuffs back on Helene and removed the twist ties from her ankles.

"All right you two. We'll go back to the station and take your statements. You can tell us why you hired a burglar to steal these crystals."

CHAPTER SIX

It proved to be a long day for the duo. When they finally returned to the office, the sun was already on the rise. They placed Aaron and Helene in the order's holding cells and headed to their temporary desks to fill out reports.

Trig sighed. "What a time. We started yesterday in Vermont, you got to rappel down a building, I got to be a chicken, and we caught criminals."

Stephanie looked thoughtfully at him across the desks. "I don't know. The story Aaron told about his wife and child—I feel for him. And his aunt simply tried to help."

"They did steal from others, and they did turn me into a chicken. There should be some penalties for those crimes."

"I know. I'm only saying that I feel bad for them." She looked thoughtful. "Do you think the spell Helene planned to use would work? Do you think it could find the hit-and-run perpetrator?"

Trig thought about it for a moment. "Yes, I do." He looked closely at her. "Wait a minute. I know that look. You plan to ask the Chief if he'll let her do it."

Stephanie simply smiled. "You know me so well. Come on. Let's see if we can do this. She can cast her spell. All we have to do is hand the information to the local police. They get to close a cold case and Aaron can have the closure he deserves."

"Yeah. Okay. Let's run it by the chief," he agreed.

After explaining their plan, Chief Yordan decided to allow Helene to perform the spell before they returned the stolen merchandise to their owners. The witch promised that the spell wouldn't damage or harm the crystals. She gave them no reason to disbelieve her.

The area surrounding the cell was crowded. Many of Herkimer's Silver Griffin agents had returned from their cases and wanted to see what was happening. Helene didn't have a problem with the audience.

A map of New York was spread in the center of her cell. Below that was a blank parchment. The Herkimer diamond crystals were positioned one at the four cardinal directions on the floor around the map. Helene held a pendulum, a chain with a pointed piece of weighted brass that directed its user to answers of questions they might ask.

The witch explained, "The pendulum will only show direction. The spell and the magic of the crystals will guide the pendulum to the exact location of our intended target." She looked at her nephew. "Unless anyone objects, I'll set the intention to finding the hit-and-run driver."

Everyone present nodded in agreement and she began her spell. Helene stood over the crystal that depicted true north. She spoke in a language that was long lost to many on Earth. After several minutes, the crystals began to glow in different colors— white for north, yellow for east, red for south, and black for west. The pendulum pulsed with a bright green glow. It began to spin at a high speed until it careened out of Helene's hand. Its point struck home near Buffalo on the map of New York. The map burned away to leave one of Buffalo on the once blank parchment. In the center, the pendulum marked the exact spot where they should be able to find the hit-and run-driver.

Chief Yordan dialed the Herkimer Police Chief, followed by the Buffalo Police Chief. He told his human counterparts where they could find their suspect driver.

A couple of hours later, Stephanie and Trig finished their reports and prepared to head home. The chief stopped them. "I just got off the phone with the Buffalo police. They say they found the driver. He had his truck repainted—a buddy of his worked at a body shop, apparently. His friend covered for him, which is why they couldn't find the vehicle. They picked them both up, the driver and his friend."

"That's good to hear, Chief." Stephanie felt a little better with that news. "Aaron had a raw deal."

"That he did," he agreed. "In fact, the owners of the crystals are willing to drop the charges. They have their property back. Nothing was damaged in the commission of the crimes, and they all wonder deep down what they would have done if their family died in a hit-and-run accident."

"What about Lodd, sir?" Trig asked.

Yordan laughed. "It's all a game to him. He'll continue to commit burglaries and we'll constantly try to keep him in custody. As long as he isn't dangerous, doesn't damage anything, and the owners get their property back, he stays one of the least of our worries here."

Trig understood. It had been a fun case, but he couldn't wait to get home.

EPILOGUE

Aaron laid flowers on the graves of his wife and child. "The magic police got him," he said as a tear fell on the grave of his little girl. "They got him."

For the first time since their deaths, he sat in peace beside their final resting place. He knew that he had been given a second chance at life, and he didn't intend to throw it away. For his wife and daughter, he would live a good life.

Stephanie and Trig finally made it to their home office in Vermont. They took turns driving so that they could each get some sleep on the way.

Their office was surprisingly busy when they entered.

Stephanie stopped and laughed when she saw their desks. Trig blushed a very deep red when he saw what she was laughing at.

On Stephanie's desk was a carton of eggs. On Trig's, there was a huge stuffed chicken. A chorus of clucking noises were heard throughout the office.

"Ha ha!" he said. "You've all had your fun." He turned to a smiling Stephanie. "What? No cock jokes?"

"Later dear." She took his hand and squeezed it gently. "Later," she said and winked at him.

Driving on I-89, a little Smart Fortwo vehicle entered the town of Saint Albans, Vermont. The small elf driver had a big smile on his face as he said, "Oh, this will be so much fun."

FINIS

AUTHOR'S NOTES

This story was so much fun to write, mainly because it is an amalgamation of many different stories that I had been writing, all squished into one.

Writing stories is a way for me to escape the real world. I love creating characters and placing them in different situations. Many times, the way I originally plan their stories turns out to be something completely different. They come to life as I write.

I hope you enjoy reading this story as much as I enjoyed writing it. Thank you for reading.

THE END TO THE DARKNESS

BY, DOMINIC NOVIELLI

It was time to fight and Jackie was ready. Forever Nycht had killed her parents and left her to be raised by her aunt, Karen, who had recently been killed by the sadistic group. Chloe Snowbanks, a supervisor for the Silver Griffins, had been a good friend to her birth mother and aunt. She took Jackie under her wing. After several months of training with magic and increasing her physical endurance, Jackie was ready for payback.

DEDICATION

To you, the fans who have picked up this book, I thank you.

CHAPTER ONE

The faint silvery scar itched and throbbed on her arm to remind her why she needed to push on with her training. It had become a part of her, a fevered compulsion that seemed bound to her very soul. She scratched absently at it as the rage and the brokenness that had spawned it surfaced as it always did when the mark stirred to life. The tide of emotion swirled around the memory of her aunt's vicious murder at the hands of the same people who'd killed her parents when she was only a baby.

It hadn't been a conscious choice on her part, but it was binding all the same. But, even knowing the dark repercussions, she couldn't regret her vow. She would do whatever it took to make sure the people who had killed her family paid for their crimes, no matter what it cost her. Chloe—her mentor and Aunt Karen's best friend—had been horrified when she'd found out, but she hadn't been there. She hadn't seen—

Jackie drew a deep breath and willed the heat in her arm to subside. The weather was already her enemy without igniting the fierce, invisible flame hungry for vengeance within.

At only eight in the morning, the sun had already begun to bake the remaining fog from the air. The temperature was eighty-one, and her once enjoyable workout had soured. She hated the heat and wished for winter to come and take her misery away. The Southern California sun continued to shine, however, burned the top of her head, and made her sweat so much that her athletic bra chafed beneath her ta-tas.

She retrieved her water jug from her daypack and took a swig to cool her dry, parched throat. Unfortunately, she was only halfway up the steep embankment from the walking path she practiced on. Every day since she'd told Chloe of her plan to see those Forever Nycht fuckers dead, she had trained diligently. The trail was a total of twenty-five miles long, and she did it every day and ran an obstacle course of her own making at the beginning and end of it. Her endurance and strength were from her dad, who was a Nycht. She still tried to come to terms with that part of herself.

"Let's get this show on the road." After a puffed breath of resignation, she grumbled and started back. The other half of her regimen waited.

Chloe had started training her in magic, which Jackie jumped into with gusto. After each day's strenuous workout, she would awaken her inner witch and let loose. If Chloe couldn't make it, she would find someone trustworthy outside of the Silver Griffins to stand in for her. Jackie thought her mentor took the training more seriously than she did—and she took it very seriously. Her intention was to not simply be a witch but the best witch she could be. Her all-day workout was painful, but it had nothing on magic practice.

"You have to clear your thoughts and only think about what you want to do." Chloe berated Jackie as she pushed herself slowly off the padded floor. They had rented a large warehouse and had installed the protective material everywhere. It was like one of those theatrical blue rooms, Jackie assumed, since all the walls and floors and even the ceiling were lined in blue cushioning.

"I am, but…" Jackie protested. "Whenever the magic feeling hits my gut, a different thought enters my head." Her brows creased together into a frown and her worried expression looked much like a vice had tried to morph her features into those of an eighty-year-old woman.

Chloe stood a moment longer before compassion eased into her features. "Okay, let's take ten. Get yourself together, and we'll try it again."

Jackie shook her head. A melancholy feeling had settled over her and she recalled days past spent with her friends—times she would never see again. She walked to the corner where they kept the water jugs and nature bars and grabbed one of each. Her inability to focus irked her because she knew her mind wasn't in the game but somehow couldn't not think about other things. She sat down to eat her snack and recalled when Chloe, her benefactor, told her the entire story about Harbinger Starscream and his group, Forever Nycht. After hearing his name, Jackie had wanted to tear his still beating heart out and feed it to him. Chloe eventually calmed her down enough to reason with her.

It was midnight when she got home. Hell, it was always midnight when she was finally able to lie down and close her eyes to once again see that giant animal pound her mother to death. At least she didn't wake up screaming anymore. But she did wake up, though, and it was always difficult to fall asleep after that image burned itself into her memory. She'd talked it over with Chloe and they had determined that the monsters were some sort of golem—a creature usually made of wood, clay, or stone, that was brought to life by magic and controlled by someone else. Who had controlled them the night her mother was killed?

It was early in the morning when Chloe rushed in and shook her awake.

"Wake up. Wake up already," she shouted into Jackie's ear after she'd tried to shake her awake for the third time. "Wow, you sleep soundly. I know you're burning both ends and straining one thing or another all day, but I still need you to wake your ass up. Now, get the fuck up before I fireball your ass!" the woman yelled, which seemed to do the trick. Jackie bounded to her feet and a couple of drops of sweat already ran down the side of her face.

"Good. I have a lead on where the Forever Nychts will be tonight!" It took Jackie a second to comprehend what she'd heard, and she wobbled a little until her eyes came into focus.

"What?" she sputtered and stumbled around as she tried to wake up. "What? You know where they'll be?" A strangled cry of surprise filled with hope erupted from the bedraggled Jackie as she rubbed the aftermath of sleep from her sore and tired eyes.

"Yes. Reg finally came through and called me to a meeting about an hour ago." She sat on the bed and patted the spot beside her in a gesture for the younger woman to sit.

Jackie's face was livid, and her eyes now reflected the same heated intensity as Chloe's as she stood and clenched her hands into fists. Her friend and teacher saw the anger and hatred that had slowly overtaken her. She couldn't—or wouldn't—let Jackie go down that one-way path to where hate and revenge filled her soul. Her love for the young witch had grown over the few months they'd been together. It was one thing to seek justice but to release the demon of revenge was quite another.

"Always remember who you are, first and foremost. The second thing to remember is how you got here. I don't mean here, as in standing in this bedroom, but here." Chloe pointed to Jackie's heart.

At first, Jackie was confused. In the silence, a picture of her mother making breakfast floated in, and then another when she was little and fell, breaking the skin on her knees and hands. She remembered her mother kissing her boo-boo's to make them better. The scenes from her life floated before her and the anger eroded and finally fell away. Eventually, she pulled herself from her reverie and realized what Chloe meant.

"I loved my mother and thought she would always be around to straighten me out." She looked at her mentor as a tight smile eased across her lips. Calmer now, she sat beside her on the bed, put her arm around her, and pulled Chloe into a tight embrace. "You have become my interim mother. I know that revenge is wrong, but it is so hard not fill myself with anger. I have a feeling that this won't be the last time you ground me when I go over-board." She pulled back from the intense hug and kissed her companion's cheek.

"I love you too, dear," Chloe replied as she returned the kiss. "Now, how about a quick bite to eat and we can start planning?" She grabbed Jackie's hand and dragged her to the kitchen.

The information received from Reg revealed that a group of Forever Nychts would be together at an address located in Villa Park. Jackie knew the area. It was where the rich people lived and where, if you had a hundred million dollars to spare, you could live in the lap of luxury. They looked the address up on the Internet, viewed the satellite map, and discerned that the backyard butted up to a hill and that there were no neighbors within shouting distance. Chloe wanted to be prepared and insisted on bringing everything and the kitchen sink. Jackie wasn't against having all they would need, but there was only so much room in a backpack.

Taut with nervous energy, her friend, who was a supervisor for the Silver Griffins, checked their gear for the fourth or fifth time—Jackie had lost count and simply waited for when it was time to leave.

"Ready?" Chloe asked her finally.

"Yes," she replied but took a second to think about what she was about to do. She asked herself yet again if she could kill someone and the answer remained a big yes. She would do what she had to do and get retribution for her family. Her stony expression had become her go-to look whenever she thought about those who had destroyed her loved ones. It was like putting on a hat.

Her companion nodded and they gathered the gear and headed to the parking lot. The routine of going to the car and driving away was soothing to Jackie. They'd followed a similar routine for a long time. Chloe had taken an extended leave of absence from the Silver Griffins to help her and to stop Forever Nycht from hurting anyone else.

They parked over a mile away, which Jackie thought was a little excessive but didn't argue. As they approached the target house, they found themselves out in the open. The only way to get anywhere close was to be invisible or drop down from a fifty-foot cliff. The house was almost as they predicted—one side backed against a mountain and it was surrounded by an eight-foot brick wall. The only other way in was through a wrought iron gate.

"If we go in under an invisibility or cloaking spell, they may have a counterspell set up on the property. If that's the case, we would be sitting ducks," Chloe explained. Jackie was silent as she contemplated the approaches in her head.

"What about that cliff?" she asked and turned her head to look at her companion.

"What about it?" Chloe scrunched her brows together. "It's way too high to levitate down, and even if we did, they might have a counterspell ready." She blew a swath of hair out of her eyes. Jackie noticed that she'd let her hair grow out more than normal since she'd showed up and wondered if she had anything to do with it.

Irritated that she'd allowed herself to be distracted, Jackie blinked a couple of times to clear her vision and her thoughts.

She needed to stay on target. That was the main problem she had with spellcraft. She had a hard time concentrating on a single thing. Getting back to their problem of entry sparked several ideas that seem to pop into her head.

"I think I have it. What about simply using a rope and climbing down the cliff?" She raised an eyebrow and waited for a response. Chloe made as if to say something, then stopped. After a moment of thought, a wide grin spread across her face.

"Huh, I can't see anything wrong with that. No magic means no countermagic." She looked appraisingly at Jackie. "The padawan outshines the master. Good job, Jackie." She patted her shoulder and they returned to the car.

It was five miles to the nearest hardware warehouse and took only a few minutes to pop in, make the necessary purchases, and return to where they'd parked previously. They both made their way to the cliff overlooking the house, but it took them three times as long to get there due to the rugged terrain and difficulty in climbing the treacherous boulders that comprised the steep incline. Sweating and breathing heavily, they finally made it to the top and both plopped on their asses. If not for the endurance and obstacle course that Jackie trained on daily, she wouldn't have made it. She was amazed at Chloe's strength and endurance but then again, she'd never seen her work out except with magic.

"How the hell did you make it up here when I barely made it?" Jackie asked her with a look of utter astonishment.

"Easy. Before you showed up, I climbed mountains as a hobby. Ever heard of Everest?" she responded with a wink. Jackie smiled and shook her head. When they were both recovered, Chloe hauled a harness out of the shopping bag and handed it to Jackie before she pulled one out for herself. After they had both clipped a couple of carabiners to each loop in the front of their harnesses, the older woman seated a large hook on top of a large boulder and another one on the rock beside it. They threaded their ropes through the individual hooks and looped the ropes around themselves.

"Here goes nothing." Jackie backed over the cliff and lowered herself slowly. Chloe grunted when she started down a minute later. About halfway down, a tingling sensation prickled over her entire body and a thick layer of air seemed to encase her. She almost lost her grip on the rope. A couple of seconds later, as she dropped another foot, she felt something slide over her. It somehow made her feel dirty like she'd had an oil shower. Taking a deep breath to calm herself, she continued. She finally stood between the cliff and the house, bent forward, and breathed deeply once again. Chloe followed a moment later.

"Is everything okay?" she asked quietly when she noticed the pained look on her trainee's face.

"Did you feel that…whatever, when you came down?" Jackie's face looked flushed.

"Those were the magic traps." Chloe patted her on the back and tried to reassure her.

"Was that dark magic?" she asked with her eyebrows raised.

"Yes and no. There was some dark magic. That slippery, yukky feeling was an indication but also, if you feel a stomach ache or smell something rotten, that might be dark magic. It comes across a little differently for everyone, but the feeling of an upset stomach and something that smells rotten seems to be a similar theme from others who have come across it," she explained as quietly as she could. She could have shrouded them in a no-sound bubble but using magic now was not a good idea.

"Okay, where to now?" Their plan had completely changed, but Chloe often said that most plans changed, and you merely had to adjust.

"Well, we need to go into the house, so let's find a way in, shall we?" her mentor suggested quietly and swept her arm out in front to usher her forward. Jackie looked at her, shook her head, and rolled her eyes. They made their way slowly to the end of the house across the backyard. They looked down the full length of the house and didn't see any windows—it was an entirely bizarre picture, and definitely seemed unnatural.

"What's up?" she asked quietly when Chloe suddenly stopped and studied the backyard.

"No windows and no doors? That's not unusual?" Chloe smirked sarcastically.

Jackie grimaced. *Now what?* She walked over to Chloe who now stood with her hands on her hips as her gaze traveled over the bleak attributes of the back.

"Well, how do we get inside—use the front door?" She chuckled because she found the situation funny for some reason.

"This sucks rhino balls," Chloe exclaimed, and Jackie laughed.

"That was an interesting way to put it. I'll have to remember that."

The woman merely gave her an innocent expression in return. A couple minutes of staring at a blank wall made them both frustrated, and when Jackie got frustrated, she got angry. She walked the couple feet to the innocuous barrier and kicked it. Her foot went into the wall without resistance and she stumbled forward. Her foot appeared to have vanished, but when she pulled it back, it reappeared. They looked at each other and simultaneously exhaled a big sigh of relief.

Thank all that's holy, a way in.

"Let me go first." Chloe gave Jackie a look that brooked no argument. They removed their harnesses and stashed them behind a low hedge around the perimeter of the backyard. Chloe dropped to her knees and poked her head into the camouflaged void. Jackie could tell that she was looking around with the way her backside wiggled, and she laughed but gummed her lips together to mute it. Her mentor finished her surveillance and backed out. She took one look at Jackie and frowned.

"Was my backside wiggling?" Her expression added a good measure of further amusement, but Jackie pressed her lips even more tightly together to keep from laughing and only nodded. Chloe gave her the hairy eyeball and shook her head.

With one more look inside the cloaked entrance, Chloe looked over her shoulder. "Let's go. The coast is clear."

"Okay, then. No pain no gain," Jackie told herself and copied her companion's entry on all fours.

CHAPTER TWO

It was dark, but a soft glow surrounded everything and was more than a little unnerving. Chloe looked about but saw nobody in what seemed to be a living room of sorts. A leather couch stood in the center with a couple of large chairs on either side and a long wooden coffee table in the center. Other than that, it offered nothing of interest. The room was featureless with plain yellow walls. One door led out, and it was closed.

A small yelp sounded from the opposite corner. "What was that?" Jackie asked. A shadow hung in that area of the room, and neither one could see what was there. "I think there's a cage in the corner with something in it."

"And how do you know that? I can't see anything." Chloe questioned her ability to see through the darkness as she peered into the shadows.

"I don't know how, but it comes in waves. I see a black and white image in my head for only a split second before it disappears, then I see it again." Jackie was as perplexed as Chloe. They walked slowly toward the yipping sound. As they approached, the outline of the cage became more distinct and soon became defined as a ghostly metal box. In the back of the enclosure, a little furry body huddled alone, shaking and yipping its displeasure.

"Oh, my God! The poor thing—what are they going to do with it?" Jackie fumed angrily. With a melodramatic swing of her arms, she batted the cage door open and rushed inside. She slowed when she reached for the small furry bundle and tried to pick it up.

"Damn, that's smarts." She cried out as the little body sprouted sharp little teeth and nipped at her hand to draw blood and Jackie's immediate respect.

"It's okay, little guy or girl. I won't hurt you. I want to help you out of here. If you don't bite me, I can do that. Are you with me, little furry dude?" She tried to calm the puppy by talking in a soothing voice. The little ball of fur leaned out of its corner to sniff at her outstretched hand. An instant later, it crawled to her and burrowed between her legs where it curled into a small ball of fluff.

"That's it, little one," Jackie cooed. She pulled the small backpack around and unzipped it to remove everything except for a couple of small towels that she left in to cover the bottom. Slowly, still murmuring sweet nothings, she picked the animal up and placed it in the pack. A little nose peeked out and sniffed a couple of times, then disappeared back into its cozy den. Jackie zipped the pack and moved it carefully to her back. Chloe had gathered the contents she had removed and put them into her pack. In silence, they exited the cage and made their way to the door.

"Okay, kiddo, let's get this show on the road." Chloe's worried frown was now followed by a grimace and pinched eyebrows. Jackie grasped the doorknob and twisted it with infinite care. She tried to not make a sound, but the hinges on the door emitted a high-pitched squeak as it opened. They flinched and froze instinctively. She turned and gave her companion an apologetic look and shrugged her shoulders.

A long hallway ran straight ahead of them and they stepped through the door. Darkness shrouded most of the narrow corridor, and they could see nothing past ten feet. Even Jackie's new ability to see provided nothing useful.

"Ready?" Chloe whispered. Jackie nodded with her lips stretched tight and tried to push down the heightened fear within her.

CHAPTER THREE

They proceeded silently down the hallway drawn onward by the sound of chanting that grew steadily louder.

"Hey, are they saying what I think they're saying?" Jackie had a horrified look on her face as she turned to Chloe.

"Yes. I had hoped I'd simply imagined it, but they are chanting to raise a demon, by the sounds of it." She stared at Jackie in utter astonishment as if she still couldn't believe it. The sing-song chorus echoed around them as if they were in a tunnel. Chloe looked again in both directions, but nothing had changed. They were still in the hallway with only blackness at both ends.

"This can't be right," Jackie said firmly. "We've walked far enough that we should be at the other end of the house. I know it's not this long." They stood in a ten-foot section of faint magical light—the same light that had radiated in the other room.

"Magic, my dear. Magic." Chloe patted her shoulder, her expression grim as she tried to think of what would keep them trapped in that corridor.

"Damn, and I thought learning physics was hard," her apprentice grumbled. She nodded and they continued toward the chanting. They must have progressed another fifty feet when Chloe felt a little chill run through her. She backed away slowly and Jackie stumbled into her.

"What, what's up, why'd ya stop?" Jackie sputtered.

"I felt some magic that I think explains the never-ending hallway." Chloe raised both hands, almost touched the ceiling, and closed her eyes. She murmured a small spell to identify what magic was at work nearby. It was a weak revealing spell that shouldn't show up on anyone's radar. She hoped.

"Wow, that's cool," Jackie said, and she opened her eyes. A white swirling cloud of magic floated above them, much like a trapped section of river which moved in one direction and then the other way. Chloe knew immediately what it was.

"It's a never-ending eddy, which creates an artificial opening into a different plane and places us in an endless walkway." She exhaled a frustrated breath and looked around. Finally, she dropped to her hands and knees and placed her head close to the floor.

"What are you doing?" a very confused and perplexed Jackie asked and raised an eyebrow. "I hope I don't have to admit you into a mental hospital. That would be a shame," she continued, and worry lines appeared on her forehead, "it really would."

"I'm looking for the source of magic that keeps this eddy open. It's probably small and protected, but it's our only chance to get out of here." A relieved student emulated her mentor and helped to search for the small magical object. They lost all track of time and had no idea how long they were at it, but finally, Jackie shouted excitedly.

"I found something, and I think it's what you're looking for." She pointed to a spot on the wall about a foot from the floor. Chloe pushed to her feet and moved closer to take a look. Sure enough, a small coin shimmered with a light reddish cast and was lodged into the wall.

"Okay, now comes the hard part." Chloe narrowed her eyes at her apprentice. "Once I break the connection between the coin and the hallway, it will inform everyone of our existence." She saw that the girl understood and nodded. Resolve flooded in and pushed her fear down.

"Well, here goes everything." With a deep breath and a little trepidation lurking in the back of her mind, she waved her wand over the magical coin and spoke the spell to break its bond to the never-ending eddy. An intense flash of bright light enveloped the hallway, followed by a sharp cracking sound like a whip would make. Their hands immediately covered their eyes against the blinding brilliance. As the light faded, they became dizzy and disoriented. Finally, they lowered their hands and opened their eyes, their balance a little unsteady, and gazed at the door.

Chloe glanced back down the hallway and saw only darkness. She turned resolutely toward their destination. It was eerily quiet, and the chanting had stopped. There was no way to know if it was because they'd successfully summoned a demon or due to her disabling the magical trap. She hoped the latter.

"The chanting stopped," Jackie whispered with a frown. Chloe nodded and sensed her trainee's uncertainty about what they'd find on the other side. After a moment of contemplation, she raised one hand and held up three fingers. She dropped one finger at a time and counted down. Jackie had adopted her stony expression that suggested coldness, but a fire had been stoked in her eyes. Chloe knew that the girl would never be the same after this. She lowered the final finger, whipped her wand, and blasted the door open into the room beyond.

Unlike the rest of the house that had been bathed in little more than a strange glow, the room they burst into was extremely well lit. It took a couple of seconds for their eyes to adjust to the brightness and when the room came into focus, Chloe wished it hadn't. Over fifty cloaked individuals stood facing them in a very large room that was over a hundred feet high and double that in length and width. Jackie shook her head and muttered. "Magic keeps changing the rules. So be it."

"Who dares come into the divine one's presence?" A deep but mesmerizing voice seemed to boom from everywhere at once. Both women scrutinized the robed gallery and Jackie immediately thought they should be singing and swaying to hymns. She admonished herself silently to stay focused.

"We do—Chloe Snowbanks and Jackie Nightshade," Chloe yelled loudly with a forcefulness that belied what she felt. She prayed silently that shouting their identity would display them in a more powerful light. At least she hoped so.

"Then you, Chloe Snowbanks and Jackie Nightshade, will suffer the consequences," the voice reverberated in response. The evil choir started to raise their arms in unison.

"Stay close to me and don't move," Chloe told her urgently as she grabbed her and pulled her to stand behind her. After a few words and a wave of her wand, a dome of light encompassed the two of them. Not a moment later, a loud crack shattered the silence and an intense beam of red magic battered Chloe's shield. She grunted and began to sink to her knees. Jackie stared, wide-eyed and shaking with fright, at her friend—no, mentor. She thought again and realized exactly what Chloe meant to her. She was family.

With a quick thought of her mother and the haunting scene of her death that played in her nightmares, determination filled her, and Jackie's fear vanished. She stepped around Chloe. "Nobody messes with my family ever again," she yelled with a ferociousness that echoed her anger. Her mentor must have heard her shout but stayed focused on the shield. She watched her writhe in pain and bucked slightly as magic careened into the dome. The powerful witch's strength was fading beneath the intensity of the attack and she gauged it would only be able to hold for a few more seconds.

"Get ready. They will break through any moment." Her teacher's breathing was labored and she barely managed to say the words. Jackie's only reaction was a single nod.

"I love you, Chloe," she whispered as she raised her arms in front of her with her palms facing the weakening shield and the choir. Within a couple of seconds, a loud tearing sound resonated through the room as the shield collapsed. A loud cry erupted from Chloe as the last of her shield disintegrated. She collapsed and laid still as her head struck the floor.

In the moment before the shield collapsed, Jackie's hands began to glow brightly. The brightness increased tenfold as the shield disintegrated. The enemy's blast of magic continued but did not reach the two women. The glowing mass that erupted from Jackie's hands had engulfed them barely in time to repel the intense onslaught. Her magic was so strong that she had to hold her eyes tightly shut in order to concentrate. The mark on her arm flared as if it had sensed her need and had waited to unleash its fury. She drew deep on the power of the blood oath, sensing that the time had come not for vengeance but for justice. Words formed in her mind unbidden, the same words she used to make the oath. She was uncertain whether she spoke them out loud or merely in her head, but it didn't matter.

"Whoever has sentenced my family and loved ones to death, I return the sentiment. I will hunt every last one of you down and kill you or find your dead body so that I may look upon it with satisfaction knowing that you will not kill again." A rush of power overwhelmed her as it surged from her core, then darkness claimed her.

CHAPTER FOUR

Consciousness crept up on Jackie like a thief in the night. The hazy release of darkness held onto her and fought to keep her in limbo. Slowly, her senses started to register. A cold breeze caressed her face and her body shivered involuntarily. Then, a rough tongue licked her nose, which crinkled from the abuse. *Is this a dream?* The question echoed in a mind still groggy from sleep.

Her awareness gradually returned as she tried to recall the past events. The last thing she remembered was fighting for her and Chloe's life. Her heart thudded rapidly as her eyes flew open, and she pushed into a sitting position. A bundle dropped onto her lap and she looked down and frowned at a young wolf pup, no larger than a rabbit, that stared up at her. She shook her head and closed her eyes to force the last vestiges of sleep away. Was the animal a figment of her imagination? It tilted its head to the side as if to determine what she was thinking.

"I think that you're that bundle of fur I thought was a dog but turned out to be you." She smiled at the entranced furball and reached out tentatively to scratch its furry head. Her rush to wake up faded as her heartbeat settled while she petted the young wolf. Jackie turned her head to look around. Chloe lay beside her, still unconscious but thankfully, her chest rose and fell evenly with her breathing. She finally realized they were on a grassy hill overlooking a forest that encircled the small clearing.

She thought she heard someone singing and noticed a swath of beautiful flowers with leaves of iridescent colors swaying to the melodious sound. No, that wasn't it. A slight breeze blew through the clearing and set the blossoms in motion, and they were responsible for the song.

"Wow!" She breathed out explosively and jerked her head from side to side to stare in real amazement.

That wasn't possible, was it? Flowers could not sing and dance. She'd thought Chloe was going crazy not long before, but maybe she was instead. A yip from her lap reminded her that the young wolf wanted attention and she scratched and tickled it absently. Jackie heard a moan and glanced at Chloe's moving body. It took a few minutes for her mentor to finally open her eyes and sit. When she did, she gasped, and her eyes widened.

"This can't be," she blurted and twisted wildly to take in the full vista.

"Why? Where are we?" Jackie asked and grimaced slightly as her furry friend rolled over and insisted she scratch her belly.

"Were in Oriceran," Chloe cried in amazement. That got Jackie's attention.

"Oh, wow. Far out. This is incredible," Jackie responded excitedly, scooped the pup from her lap, and set her down on the grass. The young wolf sniffed around to investigate all the strange smells as if tracking for the first time. Jackie brought her attention back to her friend, pushed off the ground, and clamored to her feet. The clearing was empty except for them and the pup, which somehow fell over her own feet and rolled down a small embankment. Jackie walked over to the unstable animal and picked her up before she got lost among the trees that surrounded them.

"I see our puppy turned out to be a wolf," she commented and raised an eyebrow at Jackie.

"Does that matter? She still needs to be taken care of," she responded haughtily and held the youngster protectively.

"You're right. She needs a mother, and it seems you've taken that responsibility on." With a sigh of resignation, she gave her a thin smile and a pat on the back. "It couldn't have happened to a better mommy," she added sarcastically. Jackie rolled her eyes and gave her the dirty eyeball, which made Chloe laugh.

"You'll do fine."

"Yes, I will. And don't you worry, we'll get food and water for you as soon as we can." She scratched behind the large ears. The wolf seemed to understand and yipped her approval of the plan. "I'm glad you think so." Jackie set her down gently.

Chloe took a moment to gather her thoughts. With apprehension, she turned toward Jackie. "What happened in that room after I passed out?"

"It's still a little jumbled in my head, but what I recall is that my magic created a blinding ball of energy that repulsed whatever they bombarded us with, and it blew up." She threw her hands in the air to mimic the explosion with real enthusiasm. "After that, I woke up here." She threw her arms wide and swung them in a complete circle to encompass the glade.

She suddenly stopped twirling and gasped, holding her hand to her mouth.

"What is it? What's wrong?" An exasperated Chloe rushed to get closer to Jackie like a mother protecting her child.

"Look!" Jackie point towards the Oriceran skyline. Two Moons shimmered with a slight glow as if an artist had captured the moment with soft white light. There was a slight mist in the air, which added to the splendor of the noir moment. The music from the dancing flowers played in the background as if an orchestra defined a lull between action sequences in a movie. Both women were mesmerized by the beauty and surreal quality that enveloped them.

After a moment, they turned to each other. Their mouths were wide, and they gaped like fish on land. First, Jackie smiled, then Chloe joined her. In no time at all, they laughed uncontrollably. The wolf pup sat on her butt between the two and looked from one to the other with a quizzical expression as her tongue hung out the side of her mouth. The laughter slowed but picked up again as they both looked down and saw the comical expression on their furry audience.

"Oh, my. We need to get ahold of ourselves and figure out what actually happened," Chloe wheezed between gulps of air. She held her side, which ached from all the laughter, but didn't regret the moment. Jackie was in the same shape and held her gut and breathed heavily with a satisfied smile across her lips. Finally, they managed to get it together and took a couple of deep breaths. After patting down a swath of tall dried grass to make a large comfortable seat cushion for the two of them, they sat beside one another.

"The only way I know how to make sense of what happened is to perform a little revealing magic," Chloe remarked after she'd considered the situation.

"Okay, then, do it," Jackie blurted. She wanted to get out of what felt like the fishbowl in which she felt trapped.

"It's not that simple. If you were an inanimate object, it would be a piece of cake. Since you're not, it could harm you," Chloe explained tentatively with a worried voice and a face to match. A slew of emotions danced across her features.

"I understand that I could be harmed, but it's our only clue to find out what happened, and I want to know." With an adamant stance and that stony expression again, Jackie stood her ground. "I want you to do it."

With a resigned look, Chloe shifted in front of the younger girl and placed her hands to either side of Jackie's arms below her shoulders. The pup immediately growled and drew her lips back to show her sharp little teeth.

"It's okay," Jackie told the animal in a soothing voice in an effort to calm the wolf. Eventually, she stopped growling but maintained a wary eye on Chloe.

"You have another protector. She'll come in handy when she gets a little older." The older witch grinned and looked into Jackie's eyes with deepening intensity. "Are you ready to try this? One last chance to back out."

"Ye...s, yes, I am," Jackie stuttered. She somehow felt a little less confident now that they would actually perform the magic.

"Okay, then, here we go." Chloe stood, drew Jackie to her feet, and put her hands on her temples. Within a few seconds, Jackie started to feel light-headed and stumbled. Without her mentor's strong grip, she might have fallen. She stood and stared into the woman's mesmerizing blue eyes and slowly lost herself. A pressure came to life at the bottom of her stomach and grew more intense as the magic progressed. She didn't know how much time had passed, but the pressure eventually receded, and vertigo took over so powerfully that she almost expunged the contents of her stomach. All she knew was that she spun and fell for what seemed like forever before darkness claimed her.

Jackie woke and couldn't see anything in the dim light. As her eyes adjusted, she could make out Chloe laying on a bed of leaves across from her.

"Oh, thank the stars you're awake," the woman said with relief. She stood and hurried to sit beside Jackie. The wolf pup was fast asleep, curled tightly against her in a spooning position. She finally registered the bed of leaves and full reality hit her.

"We're in a tree?" she asked in wonderment and looked around. The base of the tree must have been as large as a two- or three-bedroom apartment. Looking up, she could only see a short way before inky blackness snuffed the view entirely.

"Yes, we are. We are most certainly in a very big tree," Chloe answered with a nervous laugh.

"What's wrong?" she asked and concern wrapped around her question. She saw and felt the nervous anxiety that bled off of Chloe and it filled her with trepidation.

"Well, it's not what's wrong, per se, but what's right," she replied, her smile weak. Jackie gave Chloe her stony expression, which seemed to goad her to continue.

"Oh, boy, how do I put this? Do you remember yesterday, when I conducted the spell to reveal what magic was used and how?" A grimace crossed Chloe's feature's, and Jackie had a feeling she might not like it.

"Yes. I think I passed out. Well, I'm sure I passed out."

"You didn't pass out. You went into a waking trance." Her mentor looked at her, then at the pup, and finally at her once more. She gulped loudly and continued. "You see, the spell wasn't exactly a revealing spell, even though it revealed a fair amount." She took a couple of deep breaths. "It was actually a foretelling spell—kind of like what a gypsy would do. It is the only spell I know that would tell me the past, present, and some knowledge of the future." She stopped her narration and gave Jackie a warm, caring look. It was the loving look of a dear friend or that of a mother.

"I can take it. Please tell me," the girl implored.

"To know the future gives us the chance to change it. Not that we may want to or even need to. It's our nature to change as we gain knowledge. Even when knowing something could be good or bad." Chloe pulled Jackie into a tight hug. With a sigh and a rumble of her lips to release a blast of air, Chloe pressed on.

"Well, I learned that you are descended from a type of Nycht that protected others with extreme skill and strength. Also, your witch side is equally as formidable. In the past, Oriceran has suffered through great wars over magic, and many lost their lives. Originally, certain individuals who had immense magical abilities were asked to become a type of peacekeeper among the races. One of your ancestors was one of those peacekeepers." Chloe stopped and waited to see if she had any questions. Jackie simply breathed a sigh of relief. *That wasn't so bad.*

"Well, keep going," she chided. The woman gulped again and took a couple of deep breaths.

"Hmm." She cleared her throat. "You're part guardian witch," she blurted and almost choked on the words.

"Ah...okay, what does that mean?" Jackie shrugged and honestly didn't understand what the big deal was.

"It means you are descended from one of the most powerful witches' in Oriceran history. Nobody has heard from a guardian witch in close to ten thousand years. They vanished shortly after a great war and were never heard from again." Chloe cleared her throat. "Well, the other thing I learned was that almost all those in charge of Forever Nycht are dust. At least, most of the ones responsible for your parent's deaths." It took a moment for what she'd been told to register, and she simply waited for her mentor to finish.

"It seems that blast of raw magic was like an atomic bomb explosion, and whoever got in the way went poof." She threw her hands up and splayed her fingers to imitate an explosion.

"But who got away?" Jackie cried. "Let's go get the motherfucker right now!" she screamed. Her face had turned red, and her eyes looked like twin volcanoes ready to erupt. The young wolf snarled as she jumped and snapped at an invisible enemy when she reacted to Jackie's outburst.

Chloe waited for her to calm before she answered. When she realized that she didn't have enough information to complete the assassination of the prick who got away, she dropped her raised fists and gave her mentor an angry growl. The wolf answered with a growl of her own.

"Are you ready to hear the rest of the prediction?" Chloe's expression chastised her for getting so unhinged. With a look that would wither weeds, she nodded slowly. "And you won't go ballistic after I tell you?" The woman gave her an imploring look. She put her anger on simmer when she reminded herself that her friend was only trying to help.

"Don't kill the messenger, I take it?"

"Yes, indeed. I know you will not want to hear this, so, please stay calm." With another imploring look, she continued her synopsis of the foretelling spell.

"Harbinger Starscream escaped." Chloe winced as she said it. Jackie's anger was palpable, like an oven set to self-clean. The woman thought she might explode in an eruption of fireworks that would bathe the sky in a kaleidoscope of colors too bright to look upon. But, to her amazement, Jackie calmly bent to pet the wolf pup. It was not what she expected.

"Are you all right, Jackie?" A deep concern within her voice penetrated the air that suddenly became heavier and thicker. Jackie looked up with resignation and determination, along with that cold stare she had perfected.

"Harbinger will die. Maybe not today, or tomorrow, but soon." With that icy statement, Chloe felt a familiar chill shiver up her spine.

"Is that all you have to tell me?" the girl asked quietly. She paused and shook her head.

"I'm afraid not. The other thing that I learned was that you have a great destiny ahead of you. Your magic and strength will be needed shortly, and the tasks will be imposing and dangerous."

Something shifted and rippled deep within her. Jackie slid her palm instinctively over the silvery scar and its warmth pulsed in response beneath her palm. It offered a sense of security that came with familiarity, but she sensed that it had been harnessed by something deeper—something perhaps even darker that stirred and coalesced into new purpose.

Her quest for justice was almost done and would be when Harbinger tasted her cold wrath. But it had spawned a new and vital energy that rooted itself in her very soul.

The End

AUTHORS NOTES

Monday, October 15, 2018 9:20 AM

I'm in front of my keyboard trying to figure out what to say. What can I say other than I'm happy writing and I wish the stories could be the way I've pictured the story moving forward? In life, you have to deal with disappointment. Writing makes me very happy. As long as that feeling continues, I will write stories. Thank you again for reading all the way to these notes.

Thanks again, and keep reading!

OTHER SERIES IN THE ORICERAN
UNIVERSE:

SCHOOL OF NECESSARY MAGIC
SCHOOL OF NECESSARY MAGIC: RAINE CAMPBELL
ALISON BROWNSTONE
THE DANIEL CODEX SERIES
THE LEIRA CHRONICLES
I FEAR NO EVIL
THE UNBELIEVABLE MR. BROWNSTONE
REWRITING JUSTICE
THE KACY CHRONICLES
MIDWEST MAGIC CHRONICLES
SOUL STONE MAGE
THE FAIRHAVEN CHRONICLES
FEDERAL AGENTS OF MAGIC

**JOIN THE ORICERAN UNIVERSE FAN GROUP ON
FACEBOOK!**